IN SEARCH OF LOST LIFE

IN SEARCH OF LOST LIFE

SURAVI SHARMA KUMAR

Srishti
PUBLISHERS & DISTRIBUTORS

Srishti Publishers & Distributors
Registered Office: N-16, C.R. Park
New Delhi – 110 019
Corporate Office: 212A, Peacock Lane
Shahpur Jat, New Delhi – 110 049
editorial@srishtipublishers.com

First published by
Srishti Publishers & Distributors in 2018

10 9 8 7 6 5 4 3 2 1

Printed and bound in India

Contents

Preface

The short fiction in this collection of short stories are mostly character driven, with psychological realism drawn from the characters' motives, fears, insecurities, sense of guilt and reaction to real life dilemmas. I have used literary methods to focus on the psychological processes, and characters' mental narratives instead of simply telling a story. This book took me more than three years to complete. Seven out of the ten stories in this collection are around the life of the protagonist – Anita.

The poetics of short fiction allows the exceptional to be perceived better in relation to the ordinary. These stories converge more on the extraordinary than the quotidian without making them feel any less 'real'. The narratives concentrate on the inner landscape of characters – emotions, relationships and peculiarities of life in general. My attempt is to have the deepest emotional impact of the stories a universal appeal. 'The Night by the Tandoor' and 'The Lingering' are exploration of the emotions of a woman's feeling of guilt and insecurity. And 'This Is Anita' and 'Let's Buy you a Yoga Mat' are interior journeys of two young women.

Fiction, as we know does not simply imitate life: it gives it significance. I have used the plot, descriptions, dialogues and other literary devices of work of fiction to form and shape the everyday lives into meaningful artistically appealing stories. For instance, the representation of the everyday in the stories 'Which Reminded Her that very Moment' or 'Let's Buy you a Yoga Mat' provides it with the creation of a background on which the events unfold. The everyday life, as I have used in the stories, may also have a psychological function when it appeals to the reader's delight in the familiar – the pleasure of enjoying what is well known. Or to a voyeuristic fascination with the daily life of others – the characters they read about.

I wrote the first draft of the stories of this book during my academic years doing an MA in Creative Writing in the University of London. The writer-tutors of the MA curriculum and my cohort of the 2015 batch have read and reviewed the stories several times during the course, and with their quality inputs, I've worked on the book writing and re-writing the prose over the last two years. I hereby express my heartfelt gratitude to my teachers and my peers in the creative writing department of the Birkbeck College at Bloomsbury, London.

The role of fiction is to transcend life or the everyday life of a person into an object of reflection or beauty; and I hope the stories in this collection have achieved this in the true sense.

Dr Suravi Sharma Kumar

New Delhi

And This is Anita

I'll tell you about an incident; you may think it is nothing more than a sick love story, but it was an incident that led to my first visit to a shrink, after a good eight years of scoring A+ grades in school. But please don't ask me about every detail like on the question sheets that the receptionist of this centre hands to every person who walks in for the first time. I've filled out that questionnaire too; so in case you want to know the stuff like: whether I was ever sexually abused, what chemicals I use/used, or if I get bored easily, or feel sad every day, often, occasionally, rarely or never – you have to see the answers in the file with my name on it.

I was fourteen years old then. And like a few times before, I had a painful boil. But this time, it was located on my right buttock and in the innermost part of it. Initially, I'd ignored it for a couple of days, thinking it to be a mere abrasion from friction between the butt cheeks, considering the sultriness in the air. So, I started sprinkling a certain medicated powder on it, and also popping painkillers from Mum's medicine box. It continued for a week, and only grew worse, and one day I took a close look at the area in the bathroom. In a hand mirror I saw that the area down there, beneath my panties, appeared all flushed crimson and swollen, and it hurt like hell to touch.

Then, I was unable to sit on a chair. And that led to a day of skipping school, which prompted Mum to rush me to the doctor's. In the outskirts of the city of Kolkata, the clinic receptionist, with false eyelashes and hair like a spoonful of noodles, noted the details and asked us to wait for our turn to be seen. Among the rows of patients, seated against a background of fluorescent blue and white walls, I deposited my ass carefully on the edge of a chair as Mum fetched herself a cup of coffee from the coin-operated vending machine. After about twenty minutes of watching the muted television mounted on the wall in front of us, we walked into the doctor's room, the nameplate on the door to which read – *Consulting Surgeon Dr Vivek Kumar.*

After listening to the problem, Dr Vivek asked me a few questions, placed his palm on my forehead, examined my tongue, eyes and nails and then scribbled something on the medical forms in the white plastic folder. Against the printed heading 'Chief Complaints' he wrote:

– Pain right perineum

– Mild fever, no malaise

Then a string of letters starting with the word 'Please' that seemed to be an instruction to the nurse.

In comparison to the doctors I'd been to before, Dr Vivek looked younger with a fine goatee beard and a thick Rolex watch of shining steel with a sky-blue dial. His consulting room was in perfect order – the desk looked just polished, and each and every book on it was arranged at the perfect angle and in alphabetical sequence.

"I need to examine you," he said. The attending nurse came forth and ushered me to the examination table, where the first thing she asked me to do was take off my jeans. 'Take off your jeans and climb onto the examination table' was what the doctor had ordered. I felt as if a heavy sack of sand or something like that had fallen on my head, but before I could say a word, Mum hurried me up, helping me undo the buttons and climb onto the table. As I lay there, I thought the nurse would come over to examine me, considering the location of the problem, but, all she did was remove my panties, put my legs in a certain position, pull the curtain around me and stand by me like she was waiting for a city bus at a bus stop. Dr Vivek strode across with his gloved hands, and my mum, in keeping with her strict sense of decorum, politely left the examination area so as not to disturb him in his work. At that moment, I understood the immense power a doctor could command.

"I will have to drain the abscess," he declared as he snapped his gloves off and threw them in the bin. "Had you come earlier, I could've prescribed medication to dry it up. But now there is an accumulation of pus and this area around the buttocks can get quite messy when infected."

"When do you want to drain it?" Mum asked.

"The sooner the better."

"Okay then," Mum said without a second's thought. "Let's go for it the soonest. She has already missed a day of school."

In a span of a few minutes, the attending nurse shepherded us along a corridor into another room which had a tang of antiseptic in the air and two plump nurses, looking like twins in their uniforms, arranging trays and instruments of steel on trolleys – one trolley beside each surgical table, the tables arranged in a row in enclosures of greyish-white curtains. I changed into a light-blue gown and lay down on one of the tables while Mum stayed in the adjoining waiting room. One of the two nurses came over and darted a professional smile, then started preparing the area for the procedure, smearing it with spirit and a brown antibacterial solution, the mixed smell of which wafted into the air. Once she was done with her work, she started asking my name, about my school and all that regular stuff for a conversation. We spoke for a while as the thought of the imminent interaction with the young doctor while lying naked from my waist down kept butting my mind.

"Sister Jennifer," Dr Vivek called as he walked in, wearing a green surgical gown, a cap and a mask that lay loose below his mouth. "Are we ready?"

"Yes, doctor."

His hands went up to pull the surgical lights overhead to a certain focus of brightness, and that glare of the lights, at a certain angle, accentuated his facial features in a surreal way – the curve of his pink lips above a firm jaw line drowned me in a sea of strange emotions.

"I'll give you a little injection to numb the area and to relax you for the procedure," he said to start with. "It won't hurt any more than an ant bite."

"Okay," I mumbled.

But the injection turned out to be excruciating, and I clenched my jaws and looked up at the ceiling until the pain had passed.

A gentle chatter nearby woke me up. The dominant of the voices was Sister Jennifer's. Later, she helped me into a reclining chair in another curtained enclosure, where Mum joined me.

After about half an hour Sister Jennifer came back with a prescription, followed by Dr Vivek, now dressed in his crisp white coat and with a maroon stethoscope around his neck. He gave the prescription a once-over and added something with a few strokes of his wrist, while my gaze stayed stuck on his face like the eyes of viewers watching the climax of a blockbuster movie in the cinema. It was only when he said, 'Okay, Take care' that I realized I had been staring.

When we arrived back home, my room seemed a mess with my shoes and belts flung around and under the bed, and books and notepads cluttered on the bed and the desk. I took up a hand towel and dusted the desk with a dry towel and then wiped it with a wet one, and then brought all the books lying in various corners of the room to that gleaming surface and arranged them in alphabetical order.

Later, after dinner that night, I had a look at the prescription to see his handwriting, which was mildly overwrought but very legible, and his signature looked quite artistic with a thick upward stroke. And there, to my delight, at the bottom of the prescription, was an appointment for a follow-up visit, scheduled for a week's time.

In the days that followed, as I sat with my textbooks at my desk, or with my food at the dining table, the impression of his face didn't leave me for a moment. It stayed for weeks after the procedure, the course of antibiotics and the follow-up visit.

I changed my route to school. And started taking a detour along a road that cut through a busy patch of a commercial area to join a serene stretch of another road that led to his clinic and then past it to a bus stop, from where I could catch my school bus just metres away from Dr Vivek's office.

The first day I passed by the clinic – a modern, three-storey construction with a huge signboard in front of it containing the names of the three doctors who practised there – my eyes scanned the parking lot, the meadow in the front, the porch and the entrance of the building for any trace of Dr Vivek. Then, in spite of the disappointment of not being able to locate anything that I could relate to him, my gaze rested on his name on the signboard, which was followed by three degrees, MBBS, MS and FRCS, when a feeling of heaviness sank in my chest – a feeling that was somewhat like how I felt on a rollercoaster about to take off at full speed. That day I waited for my school bus, under a bright sky with orange streaks in it. The daylight struck the city at an extreme angle; the air was crisp, and it was a cheerful hour of the day when milkmen and newspaper hawkers went door to door delivering milk and newspapers, porters and labourers sipped teas from roadside tea vendors before heading for a day of labour in the railway station and construction sites. I counted on my fingertips the years it might have taken Dr Vivek to complete those degrees, in order to calculate his age; he couldn't be anything less than thirty-two or thirty-three years of age. I sighed at the difference.

The next day, I spotted Sister Jennifer about to enter the gate, and when I greeted her at the top of my voice she responded with equal enthusiasm. We spoke for a while – in fact, I prolonged the conversation in order to hang around the gate longer, increasing my chances of bumping into the doctor coming in or out, and that was when I saw the silhouette of a man rushing out of a silver sedan in the parking lot and into the clinic.

"Was that Dr Vivek?"

"Yes, he's in for a surgery," Sister Jennifer said.

"Does he come this early every day?"

"No, he comes earlier, by 7:30 a.m., when his first surgery slot is taken."

Next day, I got there even earlier. The scheduled time for the school bus to arrive was 8:30 in the morning, but I reached the stop at 7:30. In those days, my heart fluttered at the slightest hint of that man, even the sight of his car. There was something about the bony frame of his face – his eyes were deeper than anything else I'd seen and they burned and tore through mine in a way that I never knew was possible. On the day of the follow-up visit, a week after my drainage procedure in the clinic, when he had been explaining something to me and Mum, the intensity of a certain emotion was so great that I found myself gnawing at the inner lining of my right cheek until I had tasted the tang of blood.

One cloudy day, as I walked with an umbrella in my hand, I passed Dr Vivek by the gate.

"Oh, hi! Good morning! Off to school?" he said, responding to my greeting.

"Yes. My school bus stop is just along the road."

"Is this your regular route to school . . . ?"

"Yes."

"So? How have you been? How... have... you... been?" he said as his gaze rested on mine. A long gaze it was. If the love poems and romance quotes were true, if the eyes have a language of their own, we had a heartfelt conversation that day.

As the seconds ticked by and the conversation couldn't be stretched any further than two or three minutes, my heart-throb left. He had left, and I realized that exchanges of a few words and blazing glances only left me inflamed even more, for more. That day at school, I sat with a wet mind as a few thoughts swirled in me: I think his eyes bore the same expression of having found someone after a long search when they met mine, and, from the way he looked at me, his eyes were as thirsty for me as mine were for him. The thoughts tired me inside out. So I went to the sickroom to lie down and comfort myself for some time before I could go back to my classes.

Later, that night, I noted down his number from one of the prescriptions, and standing on the veranda beside my room, I dialled it with trembling fingers; that was just to hear his voice one last time before I went off to sleep. The morning that followed, the sky above was a patchwork of various shades of grey that hung low like a few sullen faces looking down from the sky.

Spotting his car in the distance, I slowed my pace to say a hello, or good morning or just anything. When his car approached, I saw a woman in the front seat beside him; they were both engaged in a conversation of some sort.

"Anita!" I heard someone calling from behind me.

It was Sister Jennifer at a distance on the footpath, in a brown dress and with a reddish scarf around her neck. A fine drizzle had started.

"Hi! Hey, who is that in Dr Vivek's car?" I couldn't help asking as the car passed through the gate.

"That's Dr Aisha – his wife," Jennifer said, resting a light hand on my back. "She's the gynaecologist here. And listen, I'm in a hurry as I need to prepare the first case for surgery today. Will catch up later," she said and scurried off, waving her hands at me.

"Bye."

My head started to spin, the fingers went cold, and my heart – my heart started hammering. That was when I saw Dr Vivek walking towards me in a brown rain proof jacket with a hood that had an electric blue inner lining.

"G'morning!"

"Good morning," I said. And realized he was passing me to go to the other side of the road, and as rehearsed many times before in my mind, I spoke up: "I... I wanted to have a few words with you."

"Okay! Regarding?"

"Er... I recently decided to become a doctor. Just like you. I mean, a surgeon. Do you think that's a good idea?"

"Oh! Excellent! I envy you, this stage of your life, when it's full of possibilities," he said, and our eyes met. My thoughts went over and over the word 'possibilities': possibilities of becoming a doctor, a writer or anything, and possibilities of having romantic encounter/s with him… possibilities of spending my life with him, even if –

"You should keep that in mind the very day you start medical school. Because surgeons should have –"

Just then Dr Aisha, in her white knee-length coat, showed up at the parking lot, looking at her husband with eyes that had something to say. Dr Vivek asked me to wait and went over to her.

They spoke for some time, then he lifted his hands to grab hers, saying something earnestly. They spoke to each other for a while after which she took a moment to cast a terse glance at me. They held hands for a few more minutes and then she strode towards the parking area as he kept standing where he was, resting his eyes on her, and then she got into the car and drove off.

He then remembered to come back to me saying something in a tone of winding up the conversation, and I couldn't help but glare at him angrily. He asked me something. But I didn't hear what that was. And then I ran. I ran away. When I reached the bus stop, tears welled in my eyes. As the school bus was just arriving, I jumped onto it with a promise to myself not to go to that clinic again, or care a thing about the man. I promised myself I'd have an even bigger pile of degrees after my name than his or his wife's some day.

As dusk fell at the end of that day of heavy rainfall, I lay on the recliner in the veranda beside my room from where I could see a patch of the sky that now was clear and blue. Cold currents of a certain emotion started making their way through my mind. My head seemed to have gone numb and thoughts began to chatter and swirl on their own. So much pain for no meaningful gain. Life seemed meaningless. Feeling like an insect or some other crawling creature, I called up Mina, my friend from school, because I wanted very much to tell someone something about my condition, to have a talk and share my secret with her. I asked her what she knew about 'falling in love'.

"It's something profound," she said, sounding like a wise woman.

"What do you mean?"

"A matter of something from deep within your heart. It's... it is something that, when it happens, lovers would even die for each other."

"Like in some movies and romance books?"

"Yes, movies and stories are, after all, imitations of real life," she said, sounding like our class teacher Mrs Bonnie, only not talking about maths and physics.

That day I told her that something like falling in love had happened to me, at which she squealed in horror and cheer at the same time. Even over the telephone I could see her clamp her mouth with her palm the way she did in school for every little thing that startled her the slightest bit. I described in detail how I met him, how intense my feelings for him had been from the first moment I saw him and how it kept growing more and more, or worse and worse over time.

"I can't study. I'll get a C grade this time in school," I said.

The conversation concluded with both of us swearing how true the love-at-first-sight thing was. As I put the receiver back on the cradle, a buzz in my head blurred the world around me and I went to my room to lie down on my cot. There was nobody in the house – my parents were attending a wedding that day and Deb, my brother, was out playing football with his friends in the park nearby.

I locked the door from inside and knelt down on the floor. God! Why me? Why did it have to be me in such a hopeless trap? I let myself cry. As I cried I hoped the tears would flush out the emotions within. At the end of crying for about an hour or so, my head started to feel numb. It was seven in the evening, and I thought nothing else but a good sleep would save me from this situation as that would lighten the burden and help me to wake up fresh in the morning with a clear thinking mind for the next day at school. Once again, I lay down on the cot holding on to a pillow, fighting the melancholic thoughts out of my mind and away.

But, unable to sleep, I walked into my parents' bed room looking for Mum's medicine box where I had known was her bottle of sleeping pills. A pill or two would definitely help me fall asleep and drift away from this hard reality around me at this point in time. I took the bottle of pills and water from the fridge back to my room and sitting on the bed, I gulped down the medicine as that was the only resort I had for some peace and solace at this harsh hour of my life.

When I opened my eyes after what seemed like a deep sleep, I found myself in an unfamiliar room, amidst a haze of mechanical beeps and sounds. I looked around and saw a bottle of fluid hung on a bedside saline stand which was attached to the inside of my right elbow by a plastic tube and a thick needle, and a few other wires lay hanging from my body connecting to a machine that had several graphs running across its screen and was emitting beeping sounds at a certain frequency. Then I located Mum standing by me along with Aunt Aruna – Mum's younger sister, who lived nearby and who Mum consulted for every detail in her life. I wanted to say something to her when I realised I couldn't speak properly. I wanted to lift my hands and legs – but I couldn't.

"What made you do this?" Aunt Aruna asked me in a firm tone as Mum sat down on a nearby stool with a face that was like a face with a severe eye infection.

The events of last night flared in my mind: picking up a bottle of sleeping pills and gulping down quite a few of them…

"There's another bottle of fluid left," a nurse informed Mum as she came over. "Oh, she's awake."

"When can we take her home?" Mum asked. "She just said something and moved her hands and legs a bit."

"That's a good sign. I'll tell the doctor right away," she said. "I think you'll be able to take her home tomorrow or the day after, but only after consulting the psychiatrist."

"But you've got me all wrong." I tried to speak but ended up making a few noises. "I didn't try to kill myself!" I wanted to scream "Believe me! I did take a handful of sleeping pills but that was to put myself to sleep. And that was it."

But later, when I could make the proper sounds to speak, I didn't quite get if they believed me or not. But they took me to the shrink anyway.

Let's Buy You A Yoga Mat

The car came to a halt under a tree on one side of the lane. With the corners of his eyes crinkled, his gaze that wanted to say something rested on my face. Sai and I had first met about a week back in the presence of both our mothers, and today was the first day we met on our own in a lakeside restaurant. I looked up at his bony face – the firm jaw lines gave it a sharp definition, and his dark brown eyes that had an intensity that matched what I had heard about his high flying degrees from the USA and his attitude towards life.

"Er… we just shared a long conversation. I guess I don't have to say that I enjoy your company," he said tilting his head little down as his chin wrinkled.

I let a hint of a smile on my lips.

"But, you see, I've been in the US for only two years, and not yet ready to settle down and start a family," he said. "As you know, my parents are looking for a good match to get me married. But I don't think I'm yet–"

"I understand. Life is too young yet to get stuck with one person," I managed to say this.

He grinned.

I opened the door of the standing car and stepped out.

"I think, once you've enough time after a round of dating the brides-to-be that have been lined up for you, please do let me know if you are already shacking up with someone in the US," I said, darting a compressed smile.

"Wh– what do you mean?'

"This is the best way to have fun in a conservative Indian environment, isn't it?" I had said this with a smirk and shut the door and strode away feeling his eyes on me.

After a few strides up the lane, I could feel a car approaching me. Once it cruised up beside me and braked, Sai Prakash popped out of it, his lips pursed into a firm line.

"I don't fool around with girls," he said as he came up to me. "Not even in the US. And you think I'm doing that in my parents' circle of friends? I'm not stupid," he said as his eyes went into an angry squeeze; his face remained frozen with his mouth closed tight and overall bearing a certain kind of management-school-induced authoritative air.

"Not ready for marriage but meeting girls, yes, you've explained it so well!" I said.

He looked away and then at me letting a sigh out. "I hadn't known how to say what I want to say," he said as the air around him suddenly went limp as if releasing him from its hold. He fixed his glance upon something at a distance when the expression he wore transformed into that of a nervous nerd.

"I would have asked you to marry me if... if you were slim. Or at least thinner than this," he said tilting his head to the side.

I turned my eyes and head away as the words exploded in the air.

"The next time you go to meet a girl, make sure that you get her vital statistics right – the stuff like weight, circumference of waist and hips in inches," I said, throwing back my shoulders and curling my lip, and turned away.

Once home and in my room, I closed the door. And threw myself onto the bed. "Jerk!" I shouted, pressing my face hard into a pillow. I lay there fuming, still struggling with the churning emotions and then I decided to go out for a walk. I walked long and hard, letting my anger out on the road.

Later that night, over the dining table, my mum asked, "Did you meet Sai Prakash today?"

"Who's that?" asked my younger sister, Iisha.

"I met him, Mum," I said. "He's not my type."

"What did *he* say?"

"That I'm too fat for him," I said and sank my teeth into a thick square of paneer from my plate.

"What! What did you say when he had said that?" demanded Iisha ready to break into a fist fight with someone for calling her sister fat.

"I said, I mean I was about to say, that he was a crook of the first order," I replied, meeting my mum's jaundiced eyes.

"I had to speak with ten people to get the matrimonial talk going with him. Instead of accusing him or others, you should look at yourself. Look at yourself!" snapped Mum. "It's high time you start working on your weight."

Dad sat with an expression that said he partially agreed with what Mum had said. The expression on his face seemed to say, 'But she's healthy. Not morbidly obese.' But he didn't say a word.

"You should start coming with me for Bharat Natyam dance classes," Iisha said. "Spend hours every day doing yoga and dance, you will lose weight, and be flexible like a reptile," she said, slithering her hands one over the other and grinning at me.

Iisha, my sister, was five years younger to me. She and I had been sharing the same house, the same room, the same parents, the same food, and the same blood group. But she had a slim body – and a blissful existence.

"Iisha is a gift," mother would tell her friends when we were kids. "Always busy with her own little things. Disciplined with her toys, her books, and all her knick-knacks. Doesn't ever disturb others or create any fuss about things."

Iisha's poise, her tone of voice, her choice of words, her long hair, her clothes – all of it had an elegance that was something like a trademark, and ownership that was only hers.

Now, after years of growing up together, I only arrived at the conclusion that Iisha had been born *actualized* with all the essence of life on the planet Earth, like some sort of an enlightened spirit. I had always marveled at her ability to spend her time quietly, happy with her inner self without any need of an entertainer music, TV or friends.

Putting two pillows on the head rest, I sat on the bed with my back propped up comfortably, like I was in an executive class seat on a flight. The plane took off and once up in the air it started to shudder and soon I found myself falling into a pool of water. The pool, then I realized was the lagoon of a sea. I looked all around me and there were enormous rocks on the shore, and there was a man. The man's silhouette looked like that of Mr.Swami – the sitarist who practiced music with my mum and never missed a chance to get into a lonely corner with me; I was so small then.

I woke up abruptly. I touched my face, my chest, the pillows and then looked at the wall clock. It was one at night. Pulling myself out of the dream, I lay there and realized it was another six hours before I had to go to the gym, where I had enrolled myself two months earlier just for my meeting with Sai Prakash yesterday.

My throat felt like dry paper. Iisha was sleeping peacefully on her cot next to mine. Even in her sleep, she maintained elegance; an aura encircled her.

I poured myself a glass of water.

"Hey Anita!" said Deep as I entered the gym. The gym was at one side of the sprawling campus of an Officers' club, a building from British colonial times. As Deep's father worked in the government and he was a member there, I visited the club on and off as his guest member. Deep and I had been school time buddies and two years back, we ended up joining the same office.

"Want to join me for a swim?"

"Didn't get my swimsuit."

"Borrow from someone. Tara should have a spare one."

He was right. Tara was another mini elephant, and yes, I would fit into her costume. I got a dark blue one-piece swim suit from Tara and went into the changing room. As I took off my clothes in front of the full-sized mirror, my eyes hovered over the reflection; this was something I had been avoiding ever since I had started putting on weight. The sight of the fat always made me guilty and sad. But today I dared to look at myself. The image in the mirror was a beautiful face. That was a face chiseled to perfection: thick black hair, smooth and fair complexion, light honey-brown eyes shaped like lotus petals or something as poetic as that, lips in a bow shape, a sharp nose and a well-defined jaw line (in spite of oodles of fat below the shoulders). I had it all.

The fabric of the swimming costume was ruthless; it spared not a single fold of my body: big and small bulges catapulted from nooks and corners that otherwise I covered up with carefully tailored dresses. Interrupting my own train of thoughts, I lifted my hair up to twist it into a bun to put the swim cap on, stomped out of the changing room, and dived straight into the pool, probably dispersing half the water out of it.

After the initial one stretch across the length of the pool, I drifted to the shallow side of the pool. As Deep went ahead for another couple of stretches, I forced myself to put all my might into my arms and legs and to keep swimming, burning calories as thoughts about Sai's rejection didn't leave my mind even for a moment.

"It's already seven-thirty, Anita." Deep's voice snapped me back to the present. Deep's plain looks and wheatish complexion had dimples here and there that get prominent once in a while making his face cuter. My years of association with Deep made me feel very much at ease with him, as much at ease as with any school time girl friend.

"Let's go," he said.

I stormed out of the water. Showered and changed, when I remembered seeing Deep's Facebook page where he had 'photoshopped' his face onto a body of a hulk with six or eight-pack abs.

That day at the office, I insisted that Deep teach me his photoshopping skills. We spent one whole hour practicing inserting faces on various bodies. Using his expertise with the image editing software we finished the session with me successfully inserting my face on an hourglass figure of Shilpa Shetty. The result was enticingly good, and it made me feel how I would look if I were that slim.

Later that day, before leaving his office cubicle, Deep handed me two thin booklets.

"Check these out. We're planning for an adventure trip to Rishikesh and see if you want to join us for it," he said before dashing toward the office exit.

The booklets were about a rafting company and a yoga *ashram*.

I went through the pages: there were photographs of young people in rafts sliding along with the agile currents of the Ganges River battling wild waters, rejoicing with the thrill of rafting. There were others engaged in cliff jumping and rock climbing on the Himalayan foothills. The other booklet had photographs of a sprawling house on the bank of a flowing river with verandahs running along all the sides. A prominent Basil tree stood in the middle of a yard, with 'Swami Anandaji's Ashram' written on a sign above the door. The interiors were modest. The booklets further contained images of people in various yoga positions, information about Ayurvedic tonics and concoctions, Swamiji' Satsung schedules, information of daily menus basic organic food and beds of hay that were offered. The spacious yoga hall had two large framed photographs of a radiant man in white and saffron attire – he was yoga Guru Anandaji, the founder of the ashram. Later that day at office, during our evening tea time, I passed on the booklet to my friends Tara and Reena.

The next weekend Iisha came up to me in a breezy anarkali of magenta with intricate motifs in deep green and black, her smooth hair falling on to her waist in feminine grace.

"Sis, come to my dance class today," she said brightly.

"What for?"

"We've a weekend rehearsal class for an upcoming performance in the India International Center. As part of that, we're going to have a detailed yoga session. You can join in."

"Will they allow me?"

"I'll get permission from Gurumata. No worries."

Pillion riding on Iisha's bike, holding her red cotton pouch with beadwork in one hand and resting my other hand on the tiny roundness of her shoulder, we drove through the chaos of the city traffic. It took about a half an hour to reach the school, which was only a meager four miles away.

The school was a two-storied house with a nice lawn spread lushly in the front. The entrance was marked by a Ganesha statue cut out in a monolith with a thumbprint of vermilion on the god's forehead; a few temple flowers nestled at the god's feet. We removed our slippers outside the door and stepped in. We walked up the stairs amidst clinking anklets and glass bangles to the classroom on the first floor while young students pranced up and down around us.

A bed of marigold and jasmine flowers adorned the feet of a dancing lord Shiva statue that faced the entrance of the airy classroom hall; a hanging multi-headed brass lamp burnt gracefully in front of the statue. I could feel a divine vibe I hadn't felt for a long time. The elemental forces of nature were vibrant in the place and it elevated my mind in a matter of moments.

In the middle of the hall was a white platform for the *nattuvanar* – the teacher – where lay a *mridangam* with a pair of percussion sticks and cymbals, around which gathered the girls. I joined the batch for the customary session of yoga before the dance session.In came the yoga gurus and the yoga started with the rigorous steps of Surya Namaskaram – the sun salutation – as the sun shone through the squares of the hall windows. With my years doing yoga in school, I could follow the class fairly well, and my body, to my surprise, was flexible enough to go into quite a few of the knots and twists in spite of the fat and weight. I could do a full shoulder stand and go into a half head stand with a bit of help.

When Guru Kausalya walked in, like the rest of the girls, I greeted her by touching her feet. On a silk sari of peacock green, the gold jewelry glittered on her chest as she raised her palms to bless all and walked ahead with the poise of an *apsara*.

With their toes bordered in bright red *alta* dye, dancers in their teens and early twenties stood in rows and did Surya Namaskaram in a rhythm. They all had normal body weights though quite a few of them were heavy around their bums sticking out from under their *kurtas*, which Iisha says, was an outcome of years of dance that required them to be in the half-squatting posture. In a corner at a distance a senior student led a group of five to ten year olds to the other side of the room to synchronize their '*Tha-Thai-Thai-Tha*' steps, tapping their feet on the floor, while the grown-up girls, broke into an intense movement of footwork in time with the music from the *nattuvanar*. Their anklets jingled richly, almost frantically with the precision of their footwork.

"Continuing our discussion last week on Navarasa," said the Gurumata, "Rasa is about the human state of mind. It's about what the mind feels and the expression of the feeling thereafter." The girls came over to sit cross-legged on the floor in front of her. "Our true human nature is a composite of *spirit and body.*And this body is the temple of our existence in this world, this universe...." the Guru said in a flow, in that *satsang* with her girls.

That evening, as I sat with a mug of green tea with sugar-free sweetener on my balcony, I felt like I had just experienced the beginning of a revelation. "Our body is the temple of our existence..."

The cell phone started ringing.

"Have you decided about the trip to Rishikesh?" asked Deep.

"The rafting seems exciting," I said. "But the ashram looks nicer. Have you been there before?"

"I went to the ashram with my mum about a year ago for a week," he said. "It was all about Panchakarma therapies, yoga, meditative walks, and Ayurvedic massages."

"Wow."

"And my mum lost four kilos of weight by the end of our stay."

I felt a sudden urge to be inside that ashram eating *rotis,* watery *daal,* and bottle gourd curry, trek the hilly terrain, and then go on to lie down on the massage table ; and then stand on a weighing scale to see my weight dropping down and down as each day passed by.

"So what's the plan?"

"Go for rafting and fun, followed by a stay of two days in Swami Anandji's ashram for Panchakarma treatment and massage. We're three boys – old college buddies."

"Let me find out if Tara and Reena are game for it. But I will stay for a week at least in the ashram."

The next afternoon, I called up my mum, who was in the radio station for a recording of a Sitar rendition, to borrow her car to drive down to Tara's house to plan our trip along with Deep's group. When I reached the station I found one of Mum's students with the car key waiting for me in the parking lot.

Inside the car was a stack of CDs on the front passenger seat. I went through the stack to pick up one to play, and there I came across an invitation card in a red envelope. It was an invitation to an engagement party. My eyes searched for the names of the bride and groom. And there it was: the sight of the letters stung me like a bee sting on the face. Sai Prakash was the name of the groom-to-be. My eyes darted around to check the name of the host – that is, the name of the father of the groom-to-be to cross-check if that was the same Sai. And there it was. Yes, it was the same Sai.

I drove out of the parking lot, trying desperately to blink back something in my eyes. I switched on the first CD I could grab, and pressed the accelerator hard. When I reached the party venue mentioned in the card, which seemed to be his home address, I drove round and round the place for some time. But didn't catch any glimpse of Sai.

The next day again I drove down to that place. He wasn't there. Neither was there any common friend or acquaintance with who I could strike a conversation.The next day, again I went there after my office hours. That day, as I was passing the city mall, I saw a familiar silhouette. It was Sai Prakash indeed. Clad in blue jeans and a beige t-shirt, he fell in step with a girl in a peach-orange dress flaunting a slim figure.

My head went into a spin and foot loosened on the accelerator. The car came to a halt with a series of jerks, stopping just a few feet away from a florist's flower display, making the florist squeal and storm over to my car window. As the man was showering a lashing of his tongue, I didn't even look at him as my eyes stayed stuck on Sai and the girl walking hand in hand crossing the road from the parking lot and walk towards the commercial complex.

"Back up!" cried the florist, and as I meant to hit the reverse gear, I pressed the accelerator instead and the car rammed into the flower display. The florist and a few other men around screamed. The car came to a halt and I sat there as a knot of people came over to my window.

Once safely away from the flower shop after having paid for the damages, I looked around as I had been feeling all wobbly in my head. It was about four in the afternoon, and the day light was dim with a cloud-laden sky above. The traffic was sparse. I drove around mindlessly and stopped at the same lakeside alfresco restaurant where I had met Sai weeks back. I sat there for an hour, sipping coffee and feeling something that seemed like defeat. This bitterness had nothing to do with love. I definitely wasn't in love with Sai. It was the painful rejection – this one far more intense than any other rejection I had ever faced in life. The arch of sky – over the vast lake of the city of Cyberabad began to burn with a feverish glow. A wheeling flight of water birds that seemed to be courting parties, spread over half the sky, and at a distance, the sun wobbled down to hang like a pendant from a distant tree on the lake shore.

I opened my iPad and googled 'Sai Prakash' for his online profile. I sent him a friend request and then gulped down the last part of the coffee in my cup. Farther away from my table, a couple got off a bike and went to sit at another table facing the setting sun throwing reflections on the lake waters. These lakeview restaurants of this city that had recently become cosmopolitan have actually turned into lovers' points over the years.

I shut down my iPad and strode out of the restaurant.

It was a sparkling morning in Dehradun at the foothills of the Himalayas when we seven – three girls and four boys arrived for our trip to Rishikesh. We hired two taxis to the small pilgrimage town by the Ganges. The road to Rihikesh was flooded with men in saffron clothes bearing each a bamboo pole slung over the shoulders with two water pots hanging from either end. They stopped to eat or drink or rest, and a few of them walked or danced in tandem with the religious hip-hop music of Bollywood style. Almost all of them shouted *'Bam Bam Bhole'* or *'Har Har Mahadev'*, while a few youngsters broke into a discotheque-like jig on the road blocking traffic for a while.

My mind still felt heavy from that day's car incident and what had followed. Swaying to the music, with cokes and beer cans in their hands, the rest of them in the group rejoiced to the fullest. They waved at the youngsters in saffron dancing away to glory. That was when the taxi driver reminded us about the twisting and winding mountain road ahead and we locked all the doors and sat tight.

"Here's Gangaji," said the driver after three hours, showing us the sight of the holy river and addressing it as though it were a living being, as we sat half asleep.

The river ran parallel to the winding road uphill cutting through the thick forest peppered with monkeys and scurrying animals. When we alighted with backpacks, the camping point on the river shore boasted a carpet of pebbles. I picked up a few glossy round pebbles, they seemed to be pieces of fine art as if each of them had a story of their own, an exclusive meaning of existence.

The tents of the camps stood elegant in white and blue stripes. Each tent housed two single beds, quilts with water bottles stashed around them. Food, we were told, would be local vegetarian and available at fixed times on a table set out around the tents.

The camping company organized a camp fire, and the seven of us lingered around it for the rest of that evening. As the night darkened, the boys put on some fast music and all of them broke into a jig while I sat quiet with the excuse of 'not feeling well.' We had dinner of buttery *paranthas*, cottage cheese curry, lady finger fries, lentils, and spicy hot pickles.

The next morning, after a breakfast of *poha, upma* and tea, we gathered on the pebble bed at the rafting point at eight o'clock sharp. The sound of the flowing water and gushes of mountain air muffled our voices, making it difficult to have any conversation.

As the boys arranged for a raft, we chatted with one of the water sports instructors, Harish Thapa. He was a Nepali man with accented Hindi who told us all about white water rafting – about the waves of the Ganges and various grades of rapids. Making us all stand by the fluorescent orange raft that the boys selected for us, he talked us through commands, the behaviour of the water currents and what to do in difficult situations. We then piled into the raft, and Harish released the raft into the waves. Probably perceiving my heavy mind, Harish asked me to sit in the middle of the raft and instructed me to lie down while holding onto a rope to balance my weight as and when the raft was capsizing.

The world looked surreal as the raft started taking us through the sparkling turbulence of the running water and whirling baby rapids. I pulled my thoughts away from going again and again back to that day when Sai accepted my friend request on social media and I accessed his posts, including the ones from his engagement party when I realized his fiancée – whose name was Rishika – was a law graduate and had been applying for an internship at law farms in Los Angeles where Sai lived. I downloaded two photographs of Rishika, who apparently had green eyes (green contact lenses perhaps) and used my recently acquired image editing software knowledge to photoshop a pair of enormous naked breasts onto her chest above a red skirt. I did a few more photo adjustments, like inserting a pair of butt cheeks above a pair of thick thighs on a photograph with her back towards the camera. I then uploaded the pictures to YouTube and mailed the links to all – that is to Sai's friends, and then sent the pictures to the possible law firms she might have applied to for an internship in the LA. I did all of these emails and posts from a cyber cafe far away from my home and office and from a newly created email account.

After about ten minutes of riding on the rising and plunging waves, Harish suddenly let out a shout.

"Rapid! The Wall!"

I lay down, pressing my body onto the raft and holding the rope tightly with both hands. Harish had said 'The Wall' was the most challenging rapid. At the end of a blur of violent gushes of water, when I managed to orientate myself again, I realized that Tara, Reena and three of the boys were in the water, and I was clinging onto the raft with half my body overboard. The boys crawled back onto the raft and Harish pulled Tara and Reena out of the water.

"Guys! Get ready for another rapid!" Harish shouted again in a span of about five minutes. "Roller coaster this time!"

My throat went dry at the sight of the next rapid. In a few seconds, all of us were in the water, floating downstream in our life jackets, and the raft went ahead of us. Soon, with some struggle and help from Harish and a few others, we all climbed back into the raft.

After an hour and a half of soaring and crashing through intermittent rapids, adrenaline surged in our systems and the flow of water started to appear calmer, quieter, and predictable. Soon, my mind absorbed the mood of the waters and started feeling the same.

As we approached the shores of Rishikesh, the landscape appeared dotted with temples and holy men in saffron robes doing puja rituals. In another half hour, we were back at the Triveni ghat of Rishikesh where pilgrims took holy dips in the water as lit earthen lamps swirled and flowed around them. The sky started fading and the lit lamps in the temples and on the water currents started to twinkle in the darkness. 'Ganga Aarti' – the evening ritual started soon. Clad in drenched clothes, we hurried out of the raft to change into regular clothes in a nearby public washroom. We then gathered to watch the Aarti. About a dozen young priests standing in a row blew into sparkling conches and started moving burning lamps and joss sticks, pots of fogging frankincense in circular motions as peals of brass bells undulated the air around.

In that adrenaline-hazed state of mind after a hectic day of rafting, I felt so consumed with life – the insecurities, the scare, the thrill and then the after-effects of a wrongdoing – that it overpowered me. And then, that feeling slowly started to dissipate. I drifted into a dazed state, feeling every inch of my exhausted body and crepitation of the mind. A *rishi* in a loin cloth sat on the bank of the pious waters, meditating, his face reflecting the signature of a god or a thousand gods. The expression he wore made visible hidden realities of the universe making me feel an ache to reach that kind of peace someday.

The ashram was in a high landform in the Shivpuri area of the Himalayan foothills. When we reached there, the evening chant reverberated around the ashram, resonating throughout the lanes, the trees, and the traffic. As the boys set out for a round of biking around the place, Tara, Reena, and I walked into the entry gates with a backpack and a bulky satchel each. After checking in at the front desk, the receptionist suggested that we could join the last ten minutes of the chanting before proceeding to the dining room.

We did as suggested and checked into a room with a double bed of hay. That evening we went through the collected brochures and menus of the ashram to browse through all the available options:

spiritual upliftment through meditation, Hatha Yoga practice, diet and Panchakrama for body weight management.

For some unknown inner need, for the first time in my life, after a day of physical and mental upheaval, I wanted to explore spirituality more than ever before. Tara and Reena continued with their initial wish of losing weight and went for weight loss package for ten days, but I decided to stay for three weeks, even at the risk of getting fired from my job.

After a dinner of steamed rice, bland pulses, bottle gourd curry, and green salad, we headed for our room as the rest of the people went for a meditative walk. The hollow clang of the gong woke us up at three in the morning – the Brahma Muhurta. And when we reached the meditation hall, a Guru waited for us in the hall as vibrations of collective chanting started to rise, spreading in concentric circles around us. We walked to a pile of rolled yoga mats and picked one up each. At the front of the room were quilted platforms with cushions, on one of which sat the Guru in a white dhoti. There was a statue of lord Shiva facing the chanting rows of people. The place wore the look of inexpensive prettiness and a pious vibe filled the air.

After the chanting ceased, the spacious room quickly fell silent. Then was time for meditation. I closed my eyes, as did the Guruji and the rest of the ashram guests. But images of the plunging waves of the Ganges and the face of Sai Prakash, the face of Mr Swami filled my mind. I couldn't meditate. I opened my eyes and stared at a poster on one of the walls depicting the various Chakras of our body: the Kundalini energy flow. After battle of another fifteen minutes, I rose and went to collect some literature on Kundalini energy.

Later in the morning, at sun up, Tara and Reena left for their therapies, and I decided to go walking to the riverside. I walked through the still-sleeping lane with rows of roadside stalls still half-closed and whose owners were busy cleaning and dusting their floors and display cabins. I reached the riverbank filled with the constant flow of cold puffs of air. I walked the steep steps down to the river. The ghat was now seeded with wheelbarrows showcasing colorful glass bangles and women holding baskets filled with flowers and other *puja* offerings.

After walking through the scatter of devotees and sage men in saffron robes, I sat down on a step in a deserted patch of the ghat. I sat there for a while, looking at the agile waters. The flow of the river filled me with a calm energy, and I suddenly closed my eyes, focusing my mind on my breath, like the Guru had told us during the morning meditation in the ashram.

I meditated for about half an hour and then strolled back to the ashram through the same lanes, which now bustled with people around the stalls selling brush statues of gods, myriad *puja* implements, stationery, and food. When I returned to the ashram, it was already time for our morning beverage. People stood in queues for black tea and jaggery. I joined in.

Two days passed by.

On the third day, once back from the morning trek around the Laxman Jhula and then the cottage where the Beatles lived in the 1970s when I stepped on the weighing scale, I saw I had lost two kilograms of weight. I was overwhelmed. Over the last five years, I had tried to diet on several motivation drives but without any noticeable weight loss. And now, I could see the arrow of the scale actually move downwards. Was it the walks, the yoga *asanas*, and the controlled diet over just two days? Or the riverside meditation that seemed to lighten my mind by a couple of kilograms every time I sat for an hour in quietness all by myself?

By the end of ten days, when Tara and Reena got ready to leave, my weight was down by a good five kilograms. Now, as I looked back, I knew how those five kilograms I could offload from me – three kilograms as I walked beyond the memories of Mr Swami and one kilogram as I stopped my mind going back and forth the thoughts of Sai and his fiancée, and the rest when I shed all the other general worries of life. I hoped to lose a few more kilograms during the rest of the meditative stay, ultimately ridding my mind of more and more of unpleasant thoughts and oodles of weight.

Back from my holiday at the Rishikesh Ashram, the day I stood in front of my mirror to get ready to go to office, the sight of the fabric of my old dresses sagging from my body delighted me; it delighted me more than anything else for a very long while in my life. The burgundy top I regularly wore to office was slipping down my shoulders and became too long reaching up to the middle of my thighs. When I slipped into my trousers I realized I now needed a belt to hold it to my waist, and much to my surprise, one of Iisha's leather belts that I grabbed from her almirah turned out to be right for me and gave me a good tight hold in the waist.

"No, that size is L. I'm sure it will be too large on you. Please go for this size M (medium) instead," the sales girl said as I picked up a couple of tops to try in the trial room.

Tara and Reena nodded to the words of the sales woman and I went ahead to the fitting room with 'size M' clothes.

A lot of shopping with friends for about a month had me a new cupboard-full of dresses for a new me. And quite very soon, I could see how the glances of people looking towards my direction changed. I enjoyed the appreciative looks, the admiring glances and at times the deep curious eyeing from both my male and female colleagues.

To continue with my endeavour with yoga and meditation, I insisted Deep and Tara to join me for a morning yoga class in a city park. And they did. Tara was overwhelmed by the results of yoga on me and hoped to attain similar results some day.

Under an orange-blue morning sky, we sat in rows on our mats in front of the Guru, the very first day. While following the Guru's instructions as I sat half twisted like the rest of the students and tried to move further backwards twisting my body farther, my eyes met Deep's in the next row who I realized was keenly looking at me.

I never thought even a guy as naïve and plain as him could also reserve a certain-kind-of-glance for women, I mean slim women or better looking women, or maybe pretty women. Then, never had I seen the dimples on his cheeks form so well around his mouth and the hollow of the dimple go so deep in his taut cheeks cracking into a smile – a real smile.

Which Reminded Her, That Very Moment

Betsy and Priya would be the first ones to knock on Anita's door most of the mornings to mooch a fag that they told made their bowels move. Once back from work, every evening these two girls living in a room next to Anita's, would smoke away to glory as they worked on their laptops or watched TV, or chat on the phone; and, by morning, they invariably ran out of that one last fag that could lighten their bowels for a hectic day ahead.

"You girls always seem to be shitting pebbles," said Anita.

"Shit or no shit, we have to reach office on time. So..."

Whenever, (read quite often) Anita found herself trapped in a forlorn corner, she would go to their room to spend time listening to their stories – stories about who was fooling around with whom, who said that girl or boy was like what in bed, who was caught making out with who in their office toilet, and that kind of stuff that could never bore anyone in the age group they belonged to.

On a usual Sunday afternoon, having woken up late in the forenoon, Anita opened the fridge to look for something to eat, but all that was there was two eggs and a bowl of *rajma* left over from the previous day's lunch. She took the bowl out and decided to have it spread over toasted bread in baked-beans-on-toast style. She dashed off to Priya-Betsy's room looking for a slice or two of bread. The door to their room was ajar and she went in.

"Priya! Betsy!"

Once inside, what she spotted was her friend Betsy in an upside down position with her head rested between her elbows on the floor and legs up on the wall balancing in the position.

"Is it yoga that you're doing?" Anita asked.

She was surprised and became nervous, and, abruptly came down on the floor; her face flushed, forehead beaded with sweat.

"Are you suffering from self-injury disorder? Do you want to break your spine?" Anita said.

She broke down in tears in a span of a few seconds, "I need help."

"What happened?"

"I missed my periods this time," she said clenching her palms in a pleading gesture.

"Tell me who is the culprit?"

"That's not important!"

"I want to know."

"Oogh! You've met Pankaj, na. My ex?"

"Ohh... that boy with you in the Blues the other day? He's already an ex?"

"Yes, yes!" she said. "Anita, I'm in a hot soup now. Can you help?"

"Don't panic. Buy a pregnancy test kit."

"What if it's positive?" she asked with wide eyes. "These fucking men are always in a hurry to get their hands down to your panties," she said abusively.

"Hey, I came here looking for some bread. You have any?" said Anita.

Betsy went in and came back with four slices.

"Thanks. But why were you in that inverted-erect position? Missing periods doesn't explain that."

"To abort the pregnancy in case I have conceived. Every day, I've been jumping and skipping for half an hour and then standing in that position for fifteen minutes so that it gets dislodged or something and–"

Anita slapped her forehead and pulled strands of her own hair before leaving the room.

These girls were younger, about her younger sister Iisha's age. And they were really stupid at times; unable to think of consequences – mindless sex, urinary infections after long drives. The truth is, sex got you nowhere in life. All you need is appear smart and sexy to be somewhere in life. Real sex happens in the brain.

That weekend, Betsy's pregnancy test turned out negative, and Anita decided to join the yoga classes Betsy and Priya attended. The sessions were from seven to eight in the evenings on the week days, and on the weekends from eight to nine in the mornings.

The Yoga Ashram – a single storied gabled structure had a spacious campus with a banyan tree in it that gave it a feel of an old village house. The entrance gate was painted in green and there was a flower patch and a passage lined by cobble stones that led to the reception area.

In that meditative ambience of the ashram were people from young students, to fashion designers to academicians and administrators. The yoga hall was an airy elongated room with two large framed photographs of the founder Guru and his best disciple flanking one framed photo of lord Shiva with a few incense sticks burning in the front. And, there was this white guy with Greek-God-like features, the salience of which was a pair of emerald eyes. Dressed in a loose tee and tracks in pastel colours and holding a rolled yoga mat of turquoise in his hands, he appeared to be an angel to the girls. He would always linger around in a group of foreigners – mostly white. While doing the *asanas* sitting across from her in the room he would pass Anita soft, admiring glances. His good looks and towering height made Anita hold her breath every time she caught a glimpse of him.

The other day during a morning yoga session, Anita was practicing the headstand with some help from the instructor. That day, she felt quite in control of her body and could manage to stabilize herself in a half head stand position. Balancing her weight, as she was still and erect on her elbows with her head in between them, and with her legs folded at the knees, she felt a pair of eyes on her; she couldn't resist looking towards that direction with her head still on the floor when she realized that the emerald-eyed guy had been looking her way cocking his eyebrows in appreciation. And there she was. Off she went out of balance and fell *hroom* on her back on the floor.

The instructor and the emerald-eyed guy rushed to her.

"Hey! Did you get hurt?" he asked in a non-English European accent.

The instructor asked her something and she lay there on the mattress for a while.

A couple of weeks past that incident, on a yogic prayer ceremony day in the ashram, Anita, along with her friends volunteered to do ashram duty. They got the task of distributing *prasad* and generally attending to people that gathered under the *pandal* of saffron and white. That day, Anita exchanged a few casual words with the emerald-eyed guy like 'thank you', 'welcome' and 'my pleasure'. He was George Lukas from Germany and was in India on some cultural research work, he revealed.

Thereafter every day in the ashram, he would flash his cupid smile – a mouthful of dimples that swept Anita off her feet into a world of pink and blue. At times, after the classes when they relaxed sipping herbal teas available in an iron container placed beside the Shiva statue in the entrance area, he would come over for a short conversation in broken English which seemed more like tandem exchange exercise to her than anything more.

The day Anita had performed the full head stand – the Sirshasan – holding it for a few long seconds, he came forth to congratulate and ask for a coffee treat to mark the success. That had them walking over to the nearby Madras Café along for some South Indian styled coffee from a glass and bowl of steel. This kind of an Indian coffee, he said, he had been craving to enjoy.

Another Sunday, as Priya and Betsy were held up at their office, Anita attended the class alone. After the session as Anita walked out to the auto rickshaw rank a car cruised up beside her and it was Lukas who popped his head out of the window offering her a lift.

Anita got into the car that seemed to be a second hand purchase with fading patches, scratches and dents on its body.

By and by, their friendship grew over various asanas – the bow pose, pigeon pose, eagle pose, lotus pose, and Anita became Lukas's favourite tandem exchange partner. Back in the apartment, Anita along with, Priya and Betsy started meditating on their terrace at sun rise or sun set in the hope of seeing a lightening blue light spiralling up their spines – rise of the Kundalini *shakti*.

The next weekend, Lukas, who came to the ashram on his red bicycle wearing a red helmet, gloves and sneakers, requested the three of them to spare some time for him to take him around a few monuments of Moghul times. So the next Sunday, Anita along with her friends took him to India Gate and fixed a snake charmer for him. After the exotic Indian cobra dance in tune to the snake-charmer's *been*, they fixed him a street dance performance of two dressed monkeys – Munna and Munni.

That day, as they had their hearty meal of paranthas at Chandni Chowk, Lukas took down all their cell phone numbers. And then, one evening, he called Anita up and informed that it was his birthday and asked her out for a stroll in Dilli Haat. Anita was alone in her flat reading a journal, and loneliness made her accept his invitation rather happily.

After a stroll and buying one or the other trinkets from the stalls there, followed by plates of pani puri, Anita that day found herself speaking to him in a way that she had never done to anyone for a long time, in fact, to anyone at all in her whole waking life.

Later, after a stroll around the city and having explained to him whatever history she knew about the city, they ended up in his Nizamuddin flat. The rooms were neat with rudimentary furnishing; the living room had a cane sofa set with a few yellow-green cushions on it with Indian motifs and a wooden square table at the centre.

With all his gentleness with words, he said he would get some coffee. As he went in, she looked around and went to the rack with a collection of books on Indian culture and classical music. There were books on Moghul dynasty, on the Indian Independence struggle, on Tanjour – Khajuraho temple scripture. She browsed through the pages and stopped at the one on Khajuraho erotic sculpture: being an Indian she hadn't yet been to Khajuraho or read such books yet. Suddenly she felt his presence behind her. She shut the book and turned back. He offered her a mug of coffee with a smile. He sat down on a chair with another bright yellow and blue coffee mug which she remembered, he had picked up from a pavement shop near the Red Fort the other day.

He asked in broken English heavy with German accent,

"Ever been to Khajho-arrao?"

So he had seen her looking at those erotic pictures of Khajuraho.

"No. I'll go some day. Never had the time before," she took a swig of coffee feeling his gaze on her face.

"You make good coffee," she said.

"Thank you. It's filter coffee..."

"You used a coffee machine or a South Indian coffee filter?"

"Coffee machine... I am yet to learn to use Indian filter-coffee-makers of steel..."

After a short conversation Anita rose to take leave and he offered to drop her back in his bicycle as his car was in the garage, he had informed her.

A cycle ride in the streets of Delhi under a fine drizzle threw her out of her mind. It felt so different. As the thunder grumbled above, her mind felt like a carnival of lights, laughter and sounds and possibilities in life, including romantic ones.

Anita started humming and laughing like never before.

Another weekend afternoon, after an award winning German movie and some street food inside his car on the way back, as she stepped out of his car he planted a peck on one of her cheeks.

"Goodnight," she said.

"You won't invite me in?"

"Yeah, please come in."

Inside her hostel room, as he went through all her books and magazines flung around the room, she made some tea. The evening progressed sipping tea sitting on the floor of the balcony of her room looking down at the incessant flow of cars in the street at a distance under a saffron-and-green sky.

That day they locked lips. As she went to put the mugs on the kitchen basin he followed her. He held her from her back, turned her to face him, cupped her face in his palms and planted a tender kiss. Anita knew, due to personal and social circumstances, their affair would end once the year did. But it felt so strange to find that this relation restored love, laughter and desires in her heart otherwise iced by a string of jading experiences.

Anita was ironing her office wear on a Sunday, for the week ahead enjoying a sliver of sunlight through her living room window with the curtain drawn towards one side. A knock on the door fell on her ears. There was Lukas at her doorstep. His glow in a navy shirt and fawn pant looked surreal. In fact, the room appeared surreal under the golden light of a setting sun. He carried a pouch with *tandoori* chicken *tikka* and *seekh kebabs*, a gift wrapped bottle of red wine and a book for her. She hung her ironed clothes in her cupboard hangers and then set the table with plates, spoons, forks, the bottle of wine he had brought and two Boston glasses that was a gift from someone on her last birthday. He came over to stand beside her, grabbed the bottle, yanked the cork out with his teeth and poured the amber liquid into the glasses.

After a light clinking of the glasses and a few gulps of red wine down their throats, he asked her to open the gift wrapping of the book. As she opened it, she felt all butterflies in her tummy; it was a book on the Khajuraho sculptures of love and erotica – the same book she had seen in his apartment. She left the book on the table and went to sit on the chair by the couch. He sidled up to her. And they sat browsing the TV channels, holding hands. A tenacious emotional need started bubbling inside her. His grip on her hands became firmer – palm to palm, finger to finger; his hungry gaze explored her face. In spite of all her conscious efforts, she found herself responding to each and every movement of his eyes. He came closer. And closer until she could feel nothing but his breath against her skin, and see nothing but his fair dimpled cheeks.

That night he teased, caressed and churned her like butter leading her to a grasping limpness beneath him. At the crack of dawn, the shaft of light through the window woke her. As she found Lukas next to her, she quickly sat up on the bed. She looked at him with wide eyes. He looked back. She rushed out of the bed in a reflex and sat at the edge.

"Are you alright?"

"I'm not."

"What happened?"

"Nothing. I just didn't mean to sleep with you—"

She left for the bathroom leaving the sentence in between.

"What do you mean?"

She went in the bathroom and latched the door from inside.

From inside the washroom, she heard him light a cigarette, open the door to the balcony and talk to someone. Later when she came out in a pyjama-kurta, he was still in the balcony staring at the sprawling bougainvillea with purple blossoms.

"You were not a virgin," he said.

"So?" The tone of her voice said it all.

"Luk, you did enjoy with me. You do like me. Don't you?"

"That doesn't't mean anything," she sighed dropping her hands to make a sound of exasperation, and went to the kitchenette.

"You want some tea? I'm making some for myself," she said it in such a tone of voice that created a wall around her.

"No thanks," he mumbled.

In a while, as she sipped at her tea in a pool of silence, he got dressed and quietly left.

After about one month, Priya and Betsy moved out of that flat. Betsy moved to Mumbai to join the Mumbai office of the television channel she worked for. Priya moved to Vasant Kunj to shack-up with her beau – the recent boyfriend recruit in Betsy's words.

Their flat now lay vacant. The apartment fell all silent.

The Night by the Tandoor

When she opened the door there was a man in a charcoal-grey suit, white shirt, silvery-blue tie, pocket square, and brown shoes and belt; everything shiny and new. It took her several seconds to realize that the face was familiar. Mr Ravi, it was. She couldn't help the startled look that the realization had splashed on her face. It had been two years since she had met him last. Now he offered her a small bouquet of carnations – red and white, and his hand. She received the bouquet, and his hand for a formal shake as the steel watch band rattled on his wrist. She wondered how on earth could she have missed his name on the list of invitees that Jay had prepared.

To project conviviality, she smiled. He came in with a certain whiff of cologne in the air. Standing much taller than the man in a pair of pointed court heels, she couldn't help but peer at him: he looked thinner, his frizzy hair scantier, with bald patches of his scalp shining through the strands, and his cheeks showed the pull of gravity much more than before. And whenever he spoke, fine lines came dancing around the natural folds of his face. The smile lines were perfect brackets, cut deep into his skin around a mouth that lay slightly open as a result of the large protruding front teeth in the shape of the toy spade that her daughter Maya played with.

In her slinky dust-pink dress with its knee high side slit that she had purchased for this occasion from a super brand store in Knightsbridge, she stood like a princess. Her hair, curled in a salon hours ago, bounced all over her chest and back but left a fair view of her cleavage cradled in the 'V' of the satin trimmed neck line. She ushered the man in as his gaze from under his dark bushy eyebrows rested on her face; his penetrating gaze in the depth of a seemingly deep ponder rested on her face. And there was a persistence in it that seemed to reflect the mind of a man who generally got his way through the thick and thin of life. She led him in by the veranda, through the group of guests standing with wineglasses in various attitudes of self-conscious cheer – a few of them immersed in clashes of wits, a few in crisp competitive conversation. As she walked by the people falling in step with Mr Ravi, she felt her cheeks growing hot. In a matter of seconds as they walked ahead, she looked back at her association with this man.

This man, in the early days of her association with him, she had believed him different from what he really was, had loved in him not himself but the man her imagination pictured him, a man she had sought for eagerly all her life since her teens. And, in the later days of their courtship, when she discovered her mistake, she went on loving him just the same.

At the far end of the backyard, Jay, her husband, was busy presiding over a tandoor oven in one corner of the lawn of the semi-detached East London apartment that they had purchased about two years back. For the party today – a networking get-together for Jay's corporate friends which had come after his long-awaited preferment at office, they had arranged for food through a catering service, since the number of guests who had confirmed their attendance had been nearly a hundred. They – Jay and Anita – had arranged the party area meanwhile, putting decorative lights, dainty garden furniture and arty objects in the right places and at perfect angles. Jay was so happy for himself that he wanted to give his hospitality a personal touch by cooking hot Indian snacks – tandoori kebabs and breads – himself. To this end, one of his friends from Mumbai, a chef in an Indian restaurant around the Canary Wharf area, came forth to help spice the occasion up. Two hours before the party started, bubbling with energy, this chef friend had come over with a whole lot of implements in the boot of his car – a steel bucket, terracotta pots, coal and sand – and had assembled a makeshift tandoor oven in one corner of the backyard as Jay stood watching.

Now, as she led Ravi across the lawn to Jay, she saw her husband and the chef friend busy putting the first batch of kebabs into the tandoor, which stood behind the stark white buffet table that the caterers had set at the farthest edge of the yard. The outdoor area looked perfect, duly arranged with round tables and chairs upholstered in cream and pink. As they approached, Jay caught sight of Ravi and sallied forth to hug him, and they held each other like schoolboys or long-lost best friends. She stood with a little smile as she watched them greet each other: against Jay's towering frame of six feet two inches, Ravi looked like a child tucked into one side of his chest, his eyes barely level with Jay's broad shoulders.

Jay could lift him up at a stroke with one hand, the thought crossed her mind – and probably sweep him up into the air until he begged to be released.

Leaving the two men, neither young nor old to catch up with each other, she left for the door to receive another guest. As she reached out to the door knob, she saw a flash of herself on a decorative mirror that adorned the wall leading to the door – that was an expression on her face of blended exasperation and excitation. Jay and Ravi had known each other from before; they had not been best of friends, but both been in the same cohort in a management school in the USA and became top executives in two multinational companies at about the same time. They now maintained a certain level of friendship which was not really warm but not cold either – maybe you could call the emotional temperature *tepid.* The last time they had spoken, to her knowledge, was about three years back, when she had applied for a job in Ravi's office. Thereafter Ravi had been her boss, in his swanky American corporate office. That was how she knew him.

That was for a short period of time, though.

Stealing away from the crowd, she went to sit alone on the edge of a sofa in the drawing room. She was tired from the work too. After all, she wasn't used to hosting parties. As a couple, they had not hosted one in the last five years; neither did they maintain a circle of friends or accepted many invites to dinners or parties. Jay could hardly spare the time for such socializing.

It was only this great leap in his career that had Jay into a fit of euphoria and provoked him to throw this party. Ever since the morning, she had spent her time doing up the house: cleared the corners, dusted the table-legs, the fine carved work on the flower vases, and neatened up the old fireplace that had lain covered with cardboard ever since they had moved in. In fact, she had started reviving the fireplace in preparation for the party two days back, and she had done so with the help and inspiration of an interior decoration idea from *Good Housekeeping* magazine. With a thick wire scrub, she scrubbed it with water and vinegar, as recommended in the periodical, and then, with a bristle brush, coated it with a heat-resistant soft cream paint – not because they were going to use the fireplace for coal-burning, but in order to decorate it with candles for the party. Once this was done, she went to the market and spent half a day candle-shopping, buying ivory-white candles of myriad sizes and shapes to put in the fireplace; and to decorate the mantelpiece she bought dainty crystals – dolphins, cherubs, angels, owls and cats.

As the summer sky faded with the setting sun, and the clouds dispersed, the patchouli candles she had placed on various corners of the verandah leading to the backyard glowed in all their glory and the fireplace shimmered with the rows of candles, sitting in pride of place in the hall amidst the velvet sofas. Jay sprang around the place churning out tandoori snacks for their guests. In his black trousers and white shirt with vertical navy-blue stripes, he looked taller and brighter than his usual self, and, with his light brown hair – the prominent widow's peak plastered to his scalp with hair gel – his bony face and firm jaw gleamed with the happiness that only success could bring him.

Soon the tinkle of glasses – the red wine glasses, white wine glasses, champagne flutes and sherry glasses that had lined the table on the patio – filled the room. She poured a tall glass of chilled apple cider when she found Ravi lingering around with his eyes on her. She poured a glassful of sherry into a tulip glass and offered him the drink.

"You remember my favourite drink," he said, his tone teasing yet direct, and followed by a naughty grin after a pause of a couple of seconds. It took her a moment to recover from what he had said. She hadn't realized that she had borne in mind what his favourite drink had been. Unconscious mind at play, maybe, she thought.

They walked ahead to the drawing room, and standing by the fireplace she sipped her cider as he his sherry. A tall thick-set man and a skinny woman with a boyish haircut and long gold danglers in her ears came swinging around in a drunken sally, barely missing them as they stood by the fireplace. They seemed to know her, and Ravi also knew them well. In an alcohol-induced high, she watched Ravi participate in a charged conversation with them for a while, and then slowly withdraw, and then fall quiet. He stood holding the round glass in both his hands, his eyes peering at hers, his fingers sliding over the roundness of the glass, first hesitantly, and then with a kind of firmness, as if it were one of her breasts in his hands.

Once the two voluble guests had left, a balding man with his gorgeous young wife, walked in. That was Jay's boss and soon the menfolk gathered around him to greet him. Like a true hostess, she went to stand by Jay as he welcomed the couple in. Ravi stood by with a smile on his face. Jay shepherded the couple to a nicely done table, and a good chunk of the crowd followed them.

As the pillar candles that she had carefully planted in front of the fireplace started dripping beeswax and began to smoke, she went to babysit them for a while. Kneeling, she attended to them – two of the largest among them had got tunnelled out and the wicks had gone down after about an hour of burning, making it difficult for her to relight them. She cleared the melted wax and trimmed the wick of the largest pillar that had started to smoke, and relit it, protecting the flickering flame with both hands. She then moved on to another thick candle, scooping out some wax, when she felt someone's light footfall beside her.

"Stubborn things." It was Ravi's voice. "These candles, I mean. But you want them for the beautiful illusion they create," he said as he stood beside her drinking the dregs of the sherry in his glass. He took one last gulp and put it on a side table nearby.

"Manufacturing defect, I guess," she said in a flat tone. "Burning thick candles is a messy work at times. In fact, it happens quite often with me."

"Melting candles are like melting women in a man's arms. Problems are meant to be there," he said. "I came across a similar problem once when I wanted to keep the candle burning, to keep things illuminated. But something strange happened. The candle went out, quite suddenly," he said as his hands gestured to smash and snuff a delicate flame of a candle as she kept looking at him.

"So, how have you been?" he said as he bent down to kneel beside her, as if to help her in her work. "What are you up to these days?"

"Up to nothing," she replied, her tone defensive. "Nothing in particular. Just busy with my life – my family." Her way of lowering her head as she spoke seemed to project a complex shyness and sensitivity; and he looked at her, trying to hold her glance, which kept slipping away every time he tried. The brief brushing of their gazes stirred up no deep emotion in her, but a montage of scenes from her past. The memories went flashing through her mind's eye. It was the red Kashmiri carpet in front of the fireplace that Jay bought the other day that sprang to life so many memories carefully tucked away in some corner of her mind for the last two years.

"To be busy is good but enjoying life is important," he said. "The work-life balance, as you know, is easier said than achieved."

She continued what she had been doing, collected the bits of wax and burnt wicks from the candles in her palms, then rose from the floor to bin it in the attached balcony. He too stood up. His eyes and then his steps followed her.

"How about joining the job again? Your daughter has grown a bit," he said as he lingered about, withholding emotions from his eyes.

"Not really. Maya is just six now."

He then looked at her with such intimacy, it felt like a stealthy kiss hiding away from a crowd of familiar people.

"Why did you leave so suddenly?"

"The job, you mean?"

"Yes."

"I was not well those days."

"Not well? What were you sick with?"

"I wasn't sick. It was actually a case of wrong diagnosis," she said.

"Oh really?" he said. "Misdiagnosis issues are on the rise nowadays," he went on after a pause and in a voice that seemed to have a personality of its own. She had always noticed, whenever he spoke, that he could create a certain aura about him which made his small frame look much bigger – bigger than anyone around. "The other day, one of my good friends was diagnosed with throat cancer, in a hospital right in the heart of London. For a whole month I saw him and his family suffer like hell. And then, one fine day, he received a call and a lab report declaring that he was actually free of any malignancy and–"

"My case wasn't like that."

"No?"

"It was the medicines – the treatment that precipitated an episode of disease," she said.

"That's strange," he said.

It was true. The meds had led her into an unfamiliar and exhilarating landscape that she hadn't known existed within her. That was a different dimension of her own self – a world she now feared to even look back at. That was where people cast long lingering glances at her, their eyes shrunk, forehead in frowns in some sinister suspicion. Those days, the world around her blurred away into the thin air and what existed in her life and her breath was only an emotion – a person.

"Side-effects of meds, you mean?"

"Unknown or unrecorded effects, maybe."

"Hhmm. I've read about things like that," he said. A guest couple appeared at the door demanding her attention, and she felt relieved to join them. They were leaving early, they informed, and she saw them off at the door. Ravi walked back into the backyard, and Jay she saw at a distance, was all excited over the success of the initial batches of chicken tikka kebabs. A smile formed on her lips as she saw him serving the snacks onto plates. For the first time, she saw him thrilled at such a success; success at something as small as preparing a snack for a guest.

Once the couple had left, she headed for a group of ladies one of whom she had known as the mother of one of Maya's friends at school. She would meet her almost every day while picking up Maya at three in the afternoon. As she broke into a conversation with the lady, her eyes roved over the other guests to see if all was going well. She saw Jay standing opposite a woman in a mini-dress and dainty sandals with silky straps wrapped around and above the ankles. He stood with most of his weight on his right leg as he listened to her, which she thought reflected in him a witty, independent state of mind, a carefree state of mind, maybe. He was looking a marvel today, younger and sprightly – the way he used to during their courtship, during her days of internship in the company where he worked as a manager. That was his first job before their wedding. She used to stay in a hostel with a friend in Mumbai those days.

Ravi, she spotted, was on another drink. He sat alone for a while, and then someone joined him with a drink in his hands.

About an hour whirred away.

Jay wasn't caught up with his cooking anymore and looked relaxed, spending more time with the people. As the night deepened, the pendant lights glimmered and the pottery pieces amidst the flowerpots that she had purchased only yesterday glowed under the projection of golden light from ground level, and Jay and Ravi sat in the side yard along with a group of friends.

Having an affair with a man like Ravi would never have been her idea of romance, she thought – it had to be the witch's brew of chemicals from those medicines. In fact, she hadn't associated with a man as ugly as him for a long time; and that was exactly what she had thought when she saw him for the first time in his office, sitting in his tall chair in a plush room, ready for the interview.

"It was all about the circumstances I was in," she told Ravi later, around midnight, when she sat down on a chair feeling high after two gins with orange juice, once her lady friends had left. Most of the guests had already departed by then, and Ravi had joined her, pulling a chair from a nearby table. They sat by the tandoor, the charcoal emitting a crackling sound as it cooled off.

"Those days, instead of trying to improve our relationship and change the circumstances at home, he took me to a doctor. He thought I was sick in my mind," she said, once Ravi closed in fetching a cigarette and lighter from his pockets.

"What was it that precipitated a visit to the doctor at the first place?" he asked in a casual tone muffled by the cigarette caught between his teeth.

"Marriage counselling."

"Really?" he said, dragging in a deep puff and quickly letting the smoke out. "When was that?"

"That was within six months of our wedding."

The expression on Ravi's face changed, and his eyes seemed to acquire a new depth as he started to see those days of her infidelity from a different perspective – a shift of perspective, she thought. He sat quietly with a brooding face, and then, taking a deep drag, he rested his gaze on her face and then blew the smoke slowly in her direction. Jay was nowhere in sight.

"I was in a cloud of depression in those days," she said waving the smoke away from her face. "Jay was too busy with himself. Either at the office or travelling, as you do when you have high aspirations.

Whereas, I being married and shifted into a new neighbourhood, was stuck in a forlorn house. Cut off from the world around me. Very lonely. And then… after my miscarriage, things between us started cracking up and I wanted to separate. I wanted to go away, desperately."

"How did he respond to that?"

"Maybe he was patient. Maybe he understood my loneliness. I don't know, but he decided to go for marriage counselling."

"How long?"

"We visited the counsellor, Mr Bhol, in Bloomsbury every week on Fridays for two months. He in turn referred me to a psychiatrist, for the 'instability' of my mind or mood."

"Hhmm …" Ravi uttered, his face impassive.

"And the doctor we went to put me on some medicines to help me with my feelings of melancholy. But the medicines made me feel worse. Then he put me on another set of drugs. This went on for a while, and in the meantime Mr Bhol suggested I get a job for a change of scene, to bring in a rhythm to my days and to spend time in the company of other people," she said, her gaze fixed ahead, upon nothing. "That was when I applied for that job in your office."

"Then?"

"As I didn't respond to the meds well, we decided to change the doctor and went to a second one. The new shrink prescribed a different combination of medicines."

"They didn't help you either?"

"They damaged some part of my brain, or my mind, maybe," she said in a flow. "I was in a terrible state – very unstable state of mind. That was when, I found myself swamped by a teenage-like infatuation. A massive crush on you. It was very much 'not like the adult me'. It happened only once in my life –in my early teens and thereafter, I hadn't fallen for anyone so badly, not even for Jay.For the first time in my adulthood, I started spending nights tossing on bed and thinking… thinking about ..."

"Me?"

"You of course. And generally about love and romance and how it could fill in the void in my life."

"So?"

"So it wasn't an affair of love with you."

"An affair of lust, was it?"

"No, not even that."

"Just an episode of mania?" "I'm not the kind of woman who would make love to a man while being married to another."

"What happened to you happened to me," he sighed. "I just couldn't stop thinking about you in those days. Days and nights. I too had sleepless nights just thinking–"

"I hope that feeling is gone."

"It isn't as intense. You shut down on me so cruelly."

"I had to. It was for your own good, and mine."

As he listened to her, he looked up at the star-laden sky with a quarter moon. She followed his gaze up at the sky, and, her mind conjured a smile onto the moon, like the crystal moon that Maya had hanging on her window next to her bed.

"But, I never thought that was a sickness," he said as she had been staring at the moon face. The soft smile she imagined on it changed, changed into the smile that adorned the lips of a schizophrenic who used to visit the same shrink she went to – a moon with a schizoid smile was what she now saw at the sky.

"That night on the red carpet in front of the fireplace..."

"Please stop."

"That redbrick fireplace... I still go to that hotel suite whenever I visit our Portland office. Those three days and that journey to and from Portland with you were, *and are,* the best days of my life."

They sat in a pool of silence, as their minds meandered back and forth to those days two years back and this night by the tandoor. Now, in her mind's eye, she could see herself nervously walking down the hotel staircase from Ravi's room, hoping she wouldn't bump into anyone who knew Jay and her, hoping that the people at her office would see them as nothing more than colleagues walking together, and hoping that she had taken every precaution not to carry their sin forward to the future. To her relief today, she didn't, and she had.

"Does Jay have any clue about the way things are? Between us?"

"I revealed everything to only one person – Mr Bhol my counsellor. I left it to his discretion to convey it to Jay or not, or to decide on an appropriate time for disclosure. I thought, he would know better than me when, and how, and how much to be revealed."

That was a secret revealed to Mr Bhol – she would explain to an imaginary inquisitor, that she had done it to herself as a punishment for the infidelity committed.

She heard Jay's voice – he was calling her from inside the house. She hastened towards his voice and passed by two people from the catering service dismantling the party accoutrements.

"I need to drop them back home," Jay said from a distance as two men in formal trousers and shirts with dishevelled ties tottered beside him by the door. "They're drunk and can't drive. I'm sober today, let me help them," he said.

"Okay. Carry on."

"I'll be back in an hour."

"Okay, honey … Hey, Ravi! How about you? Did you come by public transport? Or you've a chauffeur?"

"N-no. Neither."

"So come along. Join the group. I'll drop you back home. You can collect your car tomorrow."

"Okay, as you wish." He stubbed out the butt of the cigarette and went after Jay.

She waved her hands at Ravi as they crossed the lawn leaving her alone amidst the dangling lights hanging from the plum tree and the tiny cherry tree, the sapling of which she planted two years back when they had moved into this house. She breathed a deep sigh – a sigh of relief maybe. The jowly face of Mr Bhol the counsellor came floating in her mind's eye as she realized that he hadn't disclosed her secret to her husband, despite counselling him alone on a couple of occasions as part of the marriage counselling sessions they had undertaken.

The party had resolved a quandary of her life – the biggest one on that. It eased the anxiety in her mind about her status in their marriage leaving her feeling light. A smile started to crack one corner of her lips as she saw the four men leave. The tandoor was cold; the crackling sound from the burning coal was no more. She covered it with a gunny cloth before starting to climb the stairs to her bedroom to retire for the day. Once inside the room, Maya's nanny came over to her asking for her leave. She relieved her of duty and went to Maya who was sleeping peacefully on a cot surrounded by dolls and teddies. She planted a kiss on Maya's forehead and went to the dressing table and changed into her night dress. She then washed her face, removed her make-up and lay down on the master bed without switching any lights on. A few tears rolled down her cheeks; these tears she wasn't sure about.

The Lingering

The length of the walking track in the park which is a patch of reserved forest in the heart of the city was about four kilometres. Tall trees lined the paths and an occasional ant mound and wild arbours textured the place into a unique escapade to nature. Coming face to face with a lurking jungle cat, a prancing rabbit or a pea hen with broods was often a treat to walkers' eyes.

A black tracksuit with pink striped designs was what Anita was wearing for her evening jog. The sky, on that day, looked like a stained glass window of cobalt blue. The whirring sound of the wind lulled her senses, the foliage around her jostled unsettling the droves of tits perching on the branches. Stretching her body, she started with a jog, burning the initial spurt of energy. Then she continued at a fairly steady brisk walking for ten minutes or so when she felt her mind starting to swerve away to its usual rendezvous; her energy level started to fall and she slowed down to a walk. With the rhythm of her steps, her thoughts swung from the crown of her head to her toes, and back.

After about twenty minutes, seeing some people gather on a bridge, she stopped by to follow their gaze. There was a thick black cobra lying in a swamp by a water lily, its hood up and staring at the road ahead. Soon, as the shine of the fifteen-foot reptile slithered away into the undergrowth around, the onlookers dispersed and she too resumed her walk. As she tripped she looked down and found her shoelaces trailing undone, and she bent down to tie them. She hoped to complete another lap of jogging and if possible some sprinting, burning enough calories to balance out the slices of the twelve-inch meat pizza she had eaten the evening before.

"Come on! You can do it. You've already got half the way through. You will do it," she kept mumbling to herself. That was when she saw a young woman sitting on a forlorn bench in the distance. What the woman was wearing took Anita by surprise and she went ahead for a closer look: she was wearing a dress exactly like one of hers!

The dress that was so special in her life that she had preserved it in her wardrobe in spite of its tattered trims and worn threads. It was a dress she had made with her own hands – designed, tailored and embroidered all by herself. And hence, every cut and stitch of it had been etched in her memory. She had created it about seven years back. Back when her doctor had diagnosed a complication in her womb – her womb bearing a life.

Placental anomaly it was, where the umbilical cord attached to her uterus had a deformity, said the doctor. She spoke with clinical detachment yet with a pleasant tone and play of words. *You should try your best to save the nice little life within. You've to make an effort. Help the foetus survive. Will you? Are you ready for it?* Anita and

Jay nodded. They nodded to the doctor, to themselves and to the foetus – *Yes, we're there for you. We'll retrieve you.* The doctor advised balanced diet, tension free mind, a lot of rest: bed rest for the entire first trimester or maybe more and pelvic rest, which meant no sex at all until she advised further.

Anita had always been a good girl to her parents, her teachers and, after that, a good employee of a giant global enterprise. Life had been like a top spinning on a table – living in a constant sense of competition – for the next promotion, for the next award and recognition. Now this proposed long confinement to her bed was like touching the spinning top with a sudden finger. It threw her off axis.

Then, after having written ten emails and phone calls to various departments of her office, once she was done with the formalities of a long maternity leave, the bed rest left her stuck at the window of her bedroom, looking out with eyes like those of a dead fish.

In the tiny side courtyard of her house, red weaver ants stitched up the leaves of a guava sapling into enclosures for homes. Above her bedroom window in the overhanging eaves, a bunch of bees had started building a hive. Anita saw it grow each day, with the worker bees getting busy fetching nectar and returning, dancing and buzzing, after a good collection. At times on her window ledge, Anita had a little visitor: a worker bee with its body smeared with pollen and, at other times, a bee with a speck of honey on it – probably after feeding a baby bee in the hive.

During the days, hours and minutes in the 'nest' of her home, to keep her mind working -life flowing, she immersed herself in hours of television on the TV set that Jay had fixed at an appropriate angle facing her bed. At times she would meander into the pages of books or into an embroidery hoop – hemming, chain-stitching, cross-stitching, quilting. Sewing was one of her subjects in school. In those days, her mother, more than her teachers, was her guide in this art. She would spend hours with her embroidering little ponies, sparkling stars, the moon with a face, the sun with the rays and many designs more. In the sprawling house in the outskirts of the city, Anita sat fixing her eyes on the eye of a needle and running the thread through it, as if embroidery would now save her life.

Aasha – her cook, about the same age as her – would always come over to keep her company. One day, Aasha encouraged her to make a dress – a whole dress – on her own. It would keep her senses busy and hold her mind creatively, she toyed with the idea. She made a picture of the dress in pink and beige on a notebook page. She then sat for hours, downloading various designs from the internet and taking printouts. Aasha went to the market and bought the required stuff – the right fabric, trims and beads to match and coloured yarns to suit the chosen design. Then using black carbon paper Anita would draw the patterns on the fabric. With some googling help with tailoring, she cut the fabric with a pair of full-size metal scissors. And, then followed the days when Anita would sit for hours with the threaded needle, following the veins on the fabric, creating motifs of geometric precision. To keep her company, Aasha too would sit with number nine and number eleven knitting needles and wool balls of various colours to make mittens or a muffler for the upcoming baby.

Days passed. Anita absorbed herself in this task as if it would save her life.

The dress completed, she would seek other tasks to keep her mind focussed; she would try sketching, painting, anything that caught her fancy early on that morning. Every day, before her bath, she would stand in front of the mirror, naked, to measure the rise of her belly. She observed the light-blue line forming under her naval. Observed the stretching of the skin by every millimetre, which she knew would soon crack into dozens of silvery lines criss-crossing all over her abdomen.

Now standing in this park, seeing this young woman wearing that similar pink-beige dress with an embroidered scarf, had snapped an intimate cord of her heart. A few meters away from her was a smooth patch of rock surface about an inch higher than the ground level where lay a dog stretched as if dead. Anita threw a close look at the woman's face from the side: she was fiddling with a mobile phone, but wasn't playing any game or reading any text. Anita saw the depth of contemplation in her face; her demeanour reminded her of her own state seven years before. It spiralled Anita back to those days rushing her through a bygone decade of her life: the montage of events – her wedding day, the nasty flight back home from the honeymoon, many weekends spent in the office, the 'lonely' bed at night and then the day the pregnancy kit showed positive – catapulted into her mind one after the other in quick succession.

The pregnancy test had shown positive the very day she convinced herself to walk out of her marriage. Anita had told Jay about their baby. An expression filled his face that she couldn't fathom. There wasn't any overwhelming emotion; nothing to celebrate the new life within; only a delayed response. Just a few words from behind the veneer of cheeriness.

In came a world of blue: her nipples started bluing – the same fruity nipples of her younger days that she would smear with a cherry pink lipstick on first dates at college. The lips went pale, blued, dulling her face and craving weird-tasting foods that Aasha would get while running errands; sweet-and-sour delicacies and spicy munchies. The pink of her vagina blued too, and then a fine line on her lower abdomen started to form, running from her naval downwards, and started thickening in inky blue. The midriff she liked to show off over a pair of low-waist jeans now turned into a bulge to be hidden under, away from others' eyes. As if the lines from a thousand pregnancy kits stood erect and marched towards her to stripe her mind with hundreds of blue bars; the blue line on the pregnancy kit came to haunt her.

Jay's thirty-second birthday was the day Anita's first trimester of pregnancy was just over. With the doctor's due permission, they went on a dinner outing. She was blissful; he looked bright too. She wore a lightly floral, loose dress to cover her belly and feel comfortable, and he wore a dark jeans paired with a safari sports coat (a gift of hers to him). They browsed through the menu, decided what to order for the main course and a sumptuous dessert to follow. As they spoke by the restaurant window on the seventh floor watching thickening evening dusk touch the monstrous buildings and then springing up of the city lights looking like star clusters of outer space as seen on television screen, Anita found Jay's glance straying from her and their table.

His roving eyes wandered all over the place until it rested on a girl sitting two tables away from them; it was her midriff – white and smooth with an elegant curve in it much like the middle of an hour glass where his roving stopped. The girl walked about the restaurant squealing and smiling, meeting her friends. There was a ring on her belly button: a tiny little silver thing it was, with a fine turquoise stone. It sat perfectly in the concavity of her abdomen, and Anita saw there was even a little tattoo around the ring. Jay's eyes widened like a monster snake staring at its prey. His pupils opened up and from within those vital blue eyes something emerged, maybe the matrix of his mind – something transparent oozed out. Anita felt it spilling and spreading out, moving towards the girl's belly as if to touch and caress it. As the girl received it, the people around them blurred away and Anita sat there watching Jay savour that body - that pretty young thing. That was like a different dimension of the world or a dimension of their presence in that restaurant that day where she could see him savour the sensuous body, her fruity breasts and. . .

A look that was. Fully aware of her eyes on him. She sat there feeling every convolution of her mind, and the thousand and one radio voices in the air around her. The trust she had been teaching herself to build between him and her started to dwindle one more time, that very instant. The rest of the evening was quite a quiet affair. That corner of the restaurant for the rest of the night seemed to be soaked in sea water smelling of dark deep underwater weeds.

The next few days passed her by, staring at her face. Her next prenatal visit to the doctor revealed rising blood pressure and other pathologies – sugar and albumin in her urine. There was every possible sign of her stress in her body fluids. The doctor introduced new meds and advised further bed rest until the next visit.

Then, one day, an escape of red down from her womb soaked all her clothes below her waist. That day, she was wearing the self-tailored dress of pink and beige. Aasha, her only companion around the house, informed the ambulance service. The hospital staff transferred her to a bed in the casualty ward. When she opened her eyes after a thorough cleaning of her womb, and after the first bottle of blood transfusion was over and the nurse turned the IV cannula shut, removed the bag of fluid and the IV tube, she saw Jay around her hospital bed. During her stay in the hospital, he showed concern for her, her health: he ran errands, did the paperwork diligently, made phone calls to her parents and his, and donated a bottle of blood.

Later that evening, still in the haze of the sedatives, as she lay on the hospital bed receiving another blood transfusion, she observed his face keenly. Empty it was. There wasn't anything to read in it except an occasional little squeeze in his eyes. A squeeze of suspicion – suspicion about abortion, miscarriage or murder.

The woman in the park was still there. The rays of the evening sun struck the earth at a certain angle that illumed the unpaved path, her dress and the tiny white cube-like concrete constructions scattered on one side of the walking track which had toilets and security posts. There was a tall thick jackfruit tree with four fruits hanging from the branches, one of the ripe fruits of enormous size with dark brown skin and fine cracks on it, burst open and the sweet smell of jackfruit pulp wafted in the air. A gaggle of girls walked past Anita and their energy seemed to have charged the air around them. Anita went closer to her, and when she was about to say hello, she noticed marks of rolling tears down her cheeks and her eyes having a perpetual quality about them. Anita sat beside her, put her hand on her shoulder and offered a water bottle.

"Some water?"

She moved her head sideways in a polite no.

"What's your name?" asked Anita.

"Anita," she said.

"I'm Anita too! You're my namesake," said Anita overwhelmed.

The other Anita responded with a nice smile and a handshake.

She was pretty, young, and Anita instantly felt like a mature older sister to her.

"Are you all right? I can see you're weeping."

"Just feeling a little down."

"Okay. Are you pregnant?"

She nodded yes and looked away; fixed her glance on nothing in the distance and refused to look up at Anita. She refused to speak, perhaps scared of an emotional outburst in front of a stranger, perhaps never trusting a stranger to share any emotion. Perhaps ...

Anita sat beside her on the bench looking in a direction away from Anita.

"So what's the matter? Not married?"

"Married."

"Not a planned pregnancy?" She looked back at her to read her expression.

For a second time, she gave no reply and looked away. The wind had been growing steadily for quite some time now. A gust suddenly blew strands of hair from her loose ponytail onto her face. Her fingers hurried to catch the straying strands and tie them with the rest of her hair in a brown scrunchy.

"You don't want it or something?" The fleeting run of words drifted out of Anita's lips before she could think of anything against uttering those words forming that very personal question.

"Why do you want to know?" the other Anita replied with a straight face making her wordless and look away.

"I'm not sure about the baby," the other Anita said withholding all emotions.

"Not sure about its father or its fate?"

Another fleeting run of words she thought only after uttering the words.

Silence prevailed for a while.

"Okay, forget this. How long have you walked today? An hour already?"

"No, just about ten minutes. I felt so tired that I sat down."

"Come, let's go walking. Brooding and crying aren't of any help."

Anita stood up and fell into step with the other Anita.

"Let's enjoy this walk – the greens and the air," Anita said.

The other Anita's lips twisted with a hint of a smile, face softened, cheeks revitalised and eyes came back to the present. She looked better. Anita felt nice to have made a little difference to this woman, at this point in time in the park.

Anita looked up at the sky, made a wish for this woman – this woman Anita be able to give life to the bud within her. She chanted a prayer that the air of this twilight hour of the day absorbed and assimilated, and became heavier, gentler. The birds around the branches calmed, rearranging themselves on the trees. The cloud above settled cosily in the white pockets scattered all over the sky and the sun bobbed down to hang on to the line of the horizon.

Anita and Anita kept moving ahead. A couple, fellow walkers on the track, got past them triumphantly, and that prompted Anita to inspire the other Anita to keep up with them and quicken her pace. The two women started jogging and then running. Once they had passed the pair of people who had overtaken them before, they giggled away like two little girls. Peals of laughter resonated in the evening air. Then the duo started singing along the path like country bumpkins.

The *burka* of night started to veil the earth. Spotting a toilet in the distance, they went over to it. After about five minutes, Anita came out of the washroom and waited for the other Anita outside. Standing by a tree on the path, she toyed with her cell phone as she waited. About ten minutes passed and in those few minutes the whole place sank into a mire of darkness. She went to the toilet door and yelled, "Anita! Anita!" No answer. She pushed the door and it opened with a creak.

So, Anita had left. She might have gone on ahead, and may be waiting for her near the park gate. Anita walked towards the exit. The park security guards were swinging into action around her. With hand-torches sweeping like searching lights, they started whistling and asking people to leave as it was time to close.

Anita was about to reach the gate to go out when she saw Anita meters away from her, walking towards the centre of the park. With quick strides Anita followed her and yelled, "Anita!"

But the other younger Anita continued walking. Anita came face to face with a guard, standing at a road block, stopping her.

"B-but where is that woman going?"

"Who?"

"The woman who just passed by you."

"I haven't allowed anyone to cross this point at this hour!"

"But she did go past!" Anita said, agitated, finding Anita still walking, blending with the darkness, in the distance.

"Hey!" yelled a second guard to the first. The two then talked for a while as Anita kept looking for traces of Anita.

"Madam, we're going to make an announcement for Ms Anita. We'll see if there's anyone inside."

Anita heard the guard's blaring announcements and a van plied the lanes looking for Anita. But there was no response. No trace of any human being anywhere in the walking tracks -empty and winding, cutting through the forest.

The moon rode up the sapphire sky.

"Madam, we request that you leave your number with us and leave the park. If we find Ms Anita we'll inform you," one of the guards said firmly.

"No, I won't leave. . ."

Just then the silhouette of a man approached from her right side.

"Anita, what're you doing here?" he said. It was Jay – her husband!

The guards went over to him. They took him to the gate and engaged him in a conversation.

"We've all seen Ms Anita talking to herself for the last hour or so," Anita heard one of them say to Jay. "She sat beside the path and spoke and smiled and sang to herself."

"She even ran like mad, giggling like a toddler," said another.

Jay's voice was very low. She could barely hear him as he spoke to them, then came over to take Anita's hand to lead her out of the gate. Anita followed reluctantly. She saw his car parked on one side of the entrance gate, a woman emerged from inside the car. A thick woman with a tuft of black hair in a ponytail, and smile of some sort on her broad face. Her face was familiar. Unpleasantly so. Not in her white attire -her uniform, Anita thought; she was clad in flashy colours. Anita wanted to run away but Jay held her hand firmly and almost pulled her into the car. The woman came forth with a syringe. As Jay held Anita tight on the back seat of the car, the nurse introduced a drug into her blood stream. Yes, she was the nurse. That fucking woman with the pack of ampoules of injections. As she started to feel her eyelids go heavy, heart beat slow down, Anita thought she was right all those months when she suspected Jay's relationship with this woman too. Knocking her out of her senses with medicines, the duo was playing a sinister game of some sorts.

Keeping a Keen Watch over The Internet

After the short ride from the Hotel Porto Heli to the port, Anita gets out of the van and walks forward, pulling her extra-large suitcase on wheels behind her. She walks until she is standing in front of the ferry. A tall thin woman walks up to her and they begin to talk. Anita pulls a scarf out of her purse, and wraps it around her head as she speaks to shield herself from the gusts of air that roughens her hair. The woman is with a man, and was staying at the same hotel where Anita stayed, in fact in the room next door, for the last three days. A red paraglider swoops past them like a descending eagle and lands not too far away from where they are standing. As a few shadows cross her, she looks up and finds three hawks slide over the undulations of air of this island of winds – the Mykonos of Greece.

The port is on the promenade facing the sea, lined with restaurants and cafés. The rocky terrain, dotted with dazzling spots of whitewash on the cube-like constructions of the Cyclades, cradles this part of the sea in a crescent. As twenty more minutes are left until boarding starts, like many other tourists she strolls about on the coastline fringed with the frills of whitecaps lapping the shore. Admiring the panorama, looking up and about, she captures the unique rock formations on her cell phone camera from this angle at sea level. Aside from a patch of cumulus cloud on one side, the sky today is blue and bright.

Her cell phone buzzes; there is a text from her Mum.

Your phone not connecting. Received a registered envelope from Jay with a signed divorce form in it. Are you still travelling? And alone? Please call the soonest.

She never imagined that Jay would do this. That is, pull her Mum into this battle between them. Of course Mum has known him for as many years as she has, but what makes him involve her in this is beyond her comprehension. She stands there arranging her words to present it to Mum, so that she'll be able to see and feel her perspective – a wife's perspective in a marriage when they speak in a day or two.

She hopes that by the time she reaches her London home – after a whole day's journey – Mum, at her home in India, will have calmed down enough to listen to her story (over the telephone) patiently, and understand things, and respond and advise prudently, like a wise elderly lady is meant to, and not like an agitated mother.

"Excuse me!" A voice approaches her. When she looks back, she sees that it is the same woman she spoke to minutes ago. She's a young woman with East Asian facial features in a spaghetti-strapped floral dress, her man now standing with a massive backpack next to her. In a doll-like voice, the mouth full of a smile as the sunlight shines on her radiant cheeks, she asks Anita to click a photograph for them. Anita nods with a smile, and the man moves closer, to pose with her. Anita clicks.

Then the man takes the camera and clicks half a dozen photos of the lady against the vibrant waters, against the paragliders afloat high up in the air, and against the white ducks on the shore. Then, waving at her, they leave. She settles on a roadside bench to watch the seabirds shredding and lifting carcasses of seaweed that lie scattered on the shore, and tries to steady her mind, which is writhing like a worm that is fatally hurt. Has Jay found someone already? A younger, slimmer woman with an overriding sexual appetite to complement his limp libido? The thought makes her feel as if all her blood has been sucked out of her body. It was she who had initiated the divorce and pushed the paperwork forward, but, found the final plunge very hard. And now, finding Jay doing it himself makes her stomach churn.

She slides a cigarette from one of her pockets, lights it, her stare steady on the distant shore, and takes in deep puffs of smoke, feeling her brain cells spurt and crackle, using up all her mental energy. She feels like calling Jay and charging him for not sending the legal papers directly to her; after all, they've stayed separated for the whole of the last year without any phone calls, exchange of texts, or any other form of communication.

A couple of minutes pass.

Gathering her bits and pieces from the stickiness of her mind, she pulls the scarf off her head, puts her sunglasses on, and goes for a walk as the sea breeze plays with her short hair, which moves like a paddy field in a wild breeze, as do the evil-eye-bead souvenir danglers in her ears that she purchased from the winding streets of the Chora market.

As boarding commences, she walks towards the queue of hundreds of tourists, and enters the belly of the ferry through its bulbous bow. The vessel is going to go island-hopping, first to Santorini, then to a couple of small islands and finally to the port of Oia late in the afternoon, where Anita plans to catch a high speed ship to Athens. There she has a hotel booked to spend the night before heading to the airport the next day.

Once aboard, she secures her suitcase in the luggage area and looks for her seat – number nine in second-class which turns out to be a window seat. During her recent travel binge she has been opting for window seats wherever the option is available during the booking process. The windows let her unleash her mind into the air over the landscapes that swoop past. She sinks into the ergonomic chair and looks out of the window chewing over certain thoughts – thoughts that have come alive like the volcanic activity detected on the island of Santorini a couple of years back, when the molten lava grouched and grumbled underground but never burst out in the open.

The ferry moans and chugs off into the sea, forming a silvery wake. The paragliders in the distant sky appear smaller and smaller, like birds sliding in the air. The patch of cloud in the corner now spreads all over the sky, and the cloud shadows glide over the granite slopes and rock knobs of the terrain. Anita arches forward on her seat to look out and lose herself in the blue of sea and sky meeting on the distant horizon.

After what seems a long while, when she turns back to the interior of the ferry, she finds the couple she met at the port, sitting next to her in the row of seats. They exchange smiles. Then, as the lady rests her head on the man's shoulder and her eyes start to close, slowly, Anita takes her earphones out of her purse to listen to some music. The safety announcement starts to blare.

... *In the unlikely event of an emergency you'll hear a signal...*

The beads of thoughts start piling up as the meditational music of Osho begins to flow and the ferry moves ahead, showering patterns of sea water on the window glass beside her.

Jay and Anita had met during Anita's second job after her post-graduation in Delhi. By the time they met, Anita had already started working in the IT industry. She had already grown into a career woman from that starry eyed romance seeking young plump girl who would eye and fantasize almost each and every okay-looking young man she went for coffee with. At that point in time when Jay happened, she had stopped aspiring to meet any charming man and was all ready for a life of spinsterhood based on a strong career. It was a stroke of luck and, strange, not romantic turn of events that they became good friends; at her age of thirty. And, the friendship turned into matrimony when Anita once fell sick in the paying guest accommodation she had been staying in and Jay took her to the hospital and got her admitted. That's how he met her parents and brother for the first time.

From the office cubicles to coffee shops and then from coffee shops to dinners together and then to their apartment dining table – the journey of their 'love story' was like any other uncomplicated, boring stories you come across in everyday life.

The ferry starts to moan hard. She looks around. The sound wakes the people napping beside her. The announcement says they're approaching an island. Landforms covered with heaps of hard, black magma, and beaches of red and black sand come into view. Soon the ferry ploughs its way through a lagoon containing black water; the dark colour of which is due to the reflection of the towering, vertical cliffs and high heaps of lava all around. The vessel slips out of the lagoon, and a red sand beach comes into view. The blackness against the red sand, the blue of the sky, and the azure of distant water creates the right harmony of colours for a beautiful landscape painting or photograph, she ponders.

The ferry comes to a halt beside a moored ship with a chestnut-brown body with fine carvings, antique-style rigging, white triangular topsails and brass fixtures glittering under a sliver of sun, completing the look of a medieval vessel. Under a clear sky, hundreds of flickering rays reflecting off the water fall on the bow of the antique ship, simulating fire.

With their gadgets of photography ready in their hands, all the ferry's passengers spring out of their seats to explore Santorini, see the live volcano and, click photos with billowing fumes. Once most of the people have poured out, Anita walks out onto the deck, to see the island of molten lava. There are heaps of burnt magma without any trace of trees except for a peculiar, patchy growth of vegetation. She feels too weak to leave the boat to trudge over the bumpy surface of the island where the tourists have already started uphill making a bee-line towards the volcano, and instead she orders a can of beer before going to the washroom.

She regards herself in the mirror over the basin: a tallish woman who now looks even thinner than before – that may be due to her recent travels, as journeys always make you lose some weight (albeit temporarily, unless you stuff your belly with ice creams, cakes or mousses) – clad in a navy cold-shoulder top over brown shorts, all purchased from Chora on the day she landed on Mykonos, looking quite boyish because of the way she has done her hair. She recently cut it in a short, spiky style and added streaks of blonde. It's the second time in a year that she has experimented with her hair, the first being an attempt with extensions, when she found herself looking too feminine for her liking.

Once out of the washroom, she sits with her eyes settled on the unusual sight of the lava-covered island, its patches of red sand and peculiar rock formations. She kicks her shoes off to sit cross-legged on the seat, and finishes her beer in a couple of minutes; then, all alone, she lies down across four seats, under a clear sky. One of her legs dangles from the edge of the seat, and she lets it swing like a child would, as a montage of her life starts doing the rounds in her mind.

Two years back, on a certain night, she had an attack of migraine. That day, back from work before her usual time, she changed into a pair of deep green slacks and a white jersey, and was working on her laptop when the pain started – it seeped into her temples, over her eyelids and the arch of bones around the eyes. She popped her medicines, had a glass of juice from the fridge, and lay down on her bed. She suspected the shot of black coffee at the office and the red wine in the pub on her way home had precipitated the attack. Soon, the chemicals in the meds soothed her to sleep.

And then she was awake, there was a woman's laughter. Maybe a friend, or a friend's wife coming over for a chat? She tried to impose the possibility on her mind, but couldn't accept it. Tying her shoulder-length hair in a loose knot, she tiptoed to the door of the room from which the laughter emanated. What she saw was a nude blonde on the laptop screen, and Jay – her husband of six foot two inches – standing naked in front of the web camera. His long hairy legs in a pair of black crocs and nothing else. Her heart started to beat fast, like a bird's or a cat's. Blood rushed to her cheeks. And when Jay's head spun round, he was startled and nervously smiling. His hands dropped, and his legs straightened.

"Ohh. Y-you awake? Er... is the headache back? Uhmm... do you want medicine?"

"Who is she?" Anita confronted.

"I don't know," he said, and exited the open window of the porn site. "She just popped onto my screen as I was working late night."

Anita looked at Jay – his masculine features, the bony face and long, sharp nose were flushed with embarrassment. This was her husband whom she now knew as a man oozing a hitherto unsuspected sexuality – unfulfilled sexuality, maybe.

"Look, don't take it seriously. It's just something like masturbation. And masturbation, as we all know, is an innocuous act. It's… it's like…" he fumbled for words.

She kept her stare fixed on his face. And he stopped searching for words to explain. He put his pants on and stood there for a long while. He then ran his fingers slowly through his hair drawing it back and making the thick cowlick at his hairline and a layer of fine sweat beads on his forehead catapult under the skylight.

"How can it be? There's a live woman out there engaging in sex with you!"

"A kind of simulation of sex, not real sex," he reiterated as he shut the system down.

Now, the blare of an announcement brings her back to the ferry. She opens her eyes and finds herself lying down, with rows of people seated all around her. More people are stepping back on the deck as the ferry crew offer their hands to help them in. She sits upright, looks around at the faces as she runs her hand over her hair, and checks the time on her watch. The people, back on their seats are still busy with their cameras and iPads, inspecting photographs of the island. A few girls stand on the seats in bikinis to click selfies with selfie-sticks against the heaps of volcanic lava not far from the ferry's deck. Another group of 'eccentric-looking' boys in shorts and bare bodies with body tattoos blazing across their shoulders and backs, and a few girls in flamboyant bikinis and rings pierced through their belly-buttons, noses, even eyebrows and tongues, are sunbathing at the front of the deck.

"The ferry will now sail to a hot-water spring, about half an hour away," announces the guide. There is a call for swimmers and divers to get ready to leap into the hot water when the ferry stops at a convenient point. And then the ferry enters a darkish triangle of water between high landforms that plunge suddenly downward in near-vertical cliffs.

Anita spots the couple who were sitting next to her in the ferry coming out to the deck, the man now dressed in a swimsuit, the woman still in her dress. Pressing lotion between her hands, she starts creaming his muscular body in a circular motion, right down to his toes. Lucky man, thought Anita. She can't remember taking care of Jay or anybody else like that in her life.

People in swimsuits queue up to dive into the water. Initially she too had plans for a swim, but now she is in no mood for that.

"Hi!" It's the same Asian woman, coming over to her now that her man has dived into the sea. "Not going in?"

"No, not feeling like," Anita says, trying to sound warm, in a way encouraging conversation.

"Same here," the woman says with equal warmth, her words and appearance seeming firmer and crisper than before.

"Where are you from?" she asks.

"I live in London," Anita says. "You?"

"Hong Kong. I've graduated from a UK University. And I was in London a couple of years back."

"I'm Anita," she says, offering a hand for a handshake.

"You can call me Elissa." Anita receives her hand for a firm shake. "I was known by that name in London as no one could pronounce my Chinese name well,' she adds.

"What's your degree in?"

"Psychology..."

They speak for a while. And Anita begins to think there's a discrepancy between the way Elissa presented herself on the two previous occasions they spoke, and now. A sharp personality is coming through; maybe this is a manifestation of a woman standing on her own two feet without the supporting shoulder of a man at hand.

"Are you guys on your honeymoon?" Anita asks.

"Y-yes, sort of," she says, and smiles, her light eyes gleaming with happiness. Then, as an afterthought, she adds, "Travelling alone?"

"Yes, alone."

"Have you been here before?"

"No. First time here."

"I saw that you didn't get off at Santorini to see the live volcano?"

"Not feeling well today. Actually, the sight of those beautiful beaches made me go sick."

"Ohh! But why?"

"Something to do with my past." Anita sighs.

"Oh really?"

"Once, it was my dream to walk the Greek beaches – the red and black sand, in a red bikini–"

"With your man?" she says.

"Yeah. True. But in those days we didn't have enough money to make it here for a holiday."

Something like a hard ring forms in her throat making her pause.

"Now the money is there," she adds with effort, withholding all emotions from her face, "but the relationship isn't."

A click of her tongue and a smirk escapes Anita's lips. She tries to gulp down the ring in her throat, but it won't move, won't leave her. The smile on Elissa's lips fades away and something shadows her eyes.

"Relationships are the toughest thing in this world, aren't they? Unpredictable most of the time," says Elissa, as her light brown eyes with their sharp upward slant grow deep, and the whites of her eyes shine mysteriously at the thought of the mystery of life – maybe the thought about the possibility of things going wrong with her beloved passed her by.

"Did you have a divorce or a separation, may I ask?"

"Both. I'm just about to get my divorce," Anita says, lowering her voice.

Elissa turns around to look at her, and smiles a vivid smile. She then leans back on the railing, putting her weight on her elbows and hugging herself, knitting her fingers over her belly, and looks ahead.

"I was married for three years after a courtship of over a year. Can you imagine?" Anita says, out of a need to talk. Elissa is not from any place near Anita's home – either in London or in India; nor is she remotely connected to her circle of friends or her life; if she were, Anita would have never felt like talking to her so openly about her personal issues. Quite often, this is what makes tourists from far-flung areas share their intimate thoughts with an openness they can't enjoy with their friends and loved ones.

Elissa stays quiet, as if letting Anita's words linger about her.

"Where did you meet?" she asks.

"We were at the same school in Mumbai," Anita says.

"You said you live in London."

"Yes, we married after our graduation in Mumbai and then emigrated to London to work in the London office of an Indian software company."

"When did you emigrate?"

"It was in the year 2000."

"Oh, was it? That was the year I went to university and started living in central London," the woman says. "So we were in the same city at the same time, and for years."

Anita smiles at that. "Those were the best days of my life. Jay, my husband, and I rented a one-bedroom apartment in North London and started our own little home."

"Which street there?"

"Nelson Road, about half a kilometre from where the Northern Line ends."

"Hhmm."

"You?"

"In a hostel, near Kings Cross St Pancras."

"Where do you work now?" Anita asks.

"I work in a telecom company in Hong Kong."

"Married?"

"For six months."

"Where did you meet?"

She thought for a while and smiled a little.

"Through government matrimonial services."

"Ohh!"

"Not lucky enough to have a love story – to have met and fallen in love and then marry."

"But now you look deeply in love with him," Anita says. "What is the matrimonial service like? Is it run by the state?"

"Yes, it is," she says. "These services are for 'left-over women' only."

"What do you mean? What's a 'left-over woman'?"

"Someone like me. An over-educated, ageing, unmarried woman whom the state has to help to find a husband." She sighs. "I was one of them. Unmarried into my thirties."

"But that's pretty young for modern times!"

"Yes," she sighs. "I envy people who have a good courtship. I wasn't lucky enough. But now, listening to you, I can see that real life goes on beyond love stories and marriages. Even long-lasting love can wear off..."

"True, Elissa. It can. Love is so fragile. It can break with the slightest turbulence."

"What tore apart your relationship? Something really bad must have happened. Tell me only if you're comfortable."

"It's the usual story. Husband falling for younger woman."

"Oops. What is the age difference between the two of you?" Elissa asks.

"Less than a year," Anita says.

"Same-age marriages run this risk, I think," says Elissa. "I've seen it with quite a few couples."

"What's your difference?"

"He's one and half years older."

"Hhmm. Pretty close," says Anita. "Do stay in good shape. That matters a lot… and," she looks around and adds, "supervise his pornography."

The words uttered, surprise her own ears, as if someone possessed her for a moment and let the words out of her – maybe her subconscious mind it was.

"C… can that be an issue?"

Anita sees her husband coming over towards them.

"Here's your husband," she changes the topic. Elissa turns back to see him. With his bristle-straight wet hair plastered over his forehead, the man smiles at both of them. She hands him his clothes and a neatly folded towel with a coy smile, and then introduces Anita to him.

"I'm Myank," he says.

"Anita."

"Good to meet you." He flashes a boyish smile and goes off to the washroom. The man is shorter than Elissa – quite short for a man. Jay on the other hand is much taller and is built much stronger than Myank.

The ferry starts off again and Anita goes back to her seat. After about an hour, at lunch time, it anchors off the shore of another tiny island called Thea. Thea has a settlement of a few whitewashed cube-shaped houses, and some souvenir shops face the piers that lie parallel to one another. There are two sprawling restaurants extending their outdoor seating onto the piers.

Anita walks into a restaurant alongside a row of sailboats and yachts moored to the coastline that is bustling with tourists from the vessel she is travelling in. The entrance contains a long rectangular glass case fitted with tiny lights showcasing the variety of seafood available in there, from fried sardines to barbecued shellfish, tiger prawns, octopus and whole squid. A charcoal grill is in operation in the distance. The air is filled with the whiff of grilled food, and charged with the cacophony of tourists occupying the indoor seating area. Anita proceeds to a table on the pier and sits at a two-seater, putting her purse on the second chair. She orders a lemonade and sips it slowly until the waitress comes over again to take her lunch order. Anita looks at the menu but doesn't feel like eating anything, and ends up asking for a red wine thinking a wine will help the sudden despair that followed the texts from her mother.

The Chinese couple sit three tables away from her. Elissa's face looks fresher now, maybe after a touch of make-up and combing. And the look on her face is now soft, bashful which seemed less a reflection of the person she actually is than of the way he wants her to be. With glasses of wine, green salads and a whole grilled squid and lobster on the table, she sits toying with her cell phone as Myank reads a document of some sort. The appearance of the whole squid on their plates is almost the same as the live ones in the aquariums, and Anita feels as if both the squids, limp on their plates, might suddenly leap into life and levitate away in the air instead of water flowing in rhythmic pulses through them, pushing them ahead.

After the lunch break, the ferry speeds off. Some people start napping, some play cards while some are still sipping beer. Anita takes her shoes off and tries to relax. Then, a sudden lurch of the vessel almost throws her off her seat. Elissa and Myank, who are standing next to their seats with cups of coffee in their hands, spill the coffee on the floor. Elissa squeals and apologizes like a sweet, sensible wife. They wipe their hands with napkins, and once the ferry stabilizes they inform a cleaner, who comes by with a mop in a bucket and starts cleaning up.

Anita stands up and leaves her seat to clear the area for him to clean. She drifts into the café in the lounge area and checks out the stuff they sell, looking for something sweet and chocolaty. Burgers, croissants, pastries and cakes are stacked beside a coffee machine, and she orders a black coffee and a chocolate brownie. Seated at the only available table in the cafeteria, she sinks her teeth into the brownie, feeling the sugar inundate her jangled nerves. And as always, the cocoa-and-sugar start working wonders. A feeling of comfort fills her up and some of the tightness eases off.

The Chinese couple comes over, apologizes again for the coffee spill. Elissa comes over to sit beside her since this is the only table with an empty chair; the rest of the place is fully packed. Myank pulls up a chair from a nearby table and both of them sit gazing at the sea through the tall glass windows, his thick right arm pressing upon her round yet thin left shoulder. They look content with their existence. An ideal couple, Anita thinks. Then Myank gets up and goes out of the door, and Elissa sidles up to Anita.

"We were talking about your relationship, I mean marriage..."

"Yes," Anita sighs, "I realized he was meeting up with women through adult websites. Do you understand what I'm saying?"

Elissa looks at her and nods, her thin lips layered with bright, rose-pink lipstick now seeming slack and pouting, making her cheeks look puffy. She may be imagining herself in that situation – her husband cheating on her and womanizing around the world.

"Would you tolerate that?" Anita asks.

"It sounds scary to have a husband so sexually loose."

Both women sit quiet for some time, staring ahead at nothing, as if copying each other's gestures and mood.

Just then, another text from Mum starts beeping. But it's the one Anita has already seen. Mum must have clicked twice when sending it, she guesses. Or she may have resent it after getting no response. But what follows now is a succession of the same text – the phone beeps for about half a minute. Some technical fault, surely, given that her phone is on international roaming and has recently been through several time zones.

The noise makes Elissa arch her eyebrows and Anita tells her what the message was about.

"Don't you think if he's involving your mum in the divorce, he probably wants to check the scope of possible reconciliation?" she says this in an easy tone of voice.

"Yes. I think so..." Anita says casually, masking the sudden realization.

The point hits home in Anita's otherwise numb brain today. "Here comes your husband," she says, spotting Myank in the crowd of people walking towards them with cans of coke and a packet of crisps.

Once he had joined them, they have a casual talk about London, Hong Kong and Mumbai. An elderly white couple comes over with mouths full of smiles and they exchange pleasantries with Myank and Elissa. They sit down on a table across from the three of them.

"They're an English couple," says Elissa. "Hours back, while walking up to Santorini, we saw the man faint and sit down on a lava heap. He is diabetic, and forgot some of his medicine this morning, the lady told us. Myank got him up and helped him to sit down on a smooth surface. You might find it interesting to know that they are ex-husband and wife. They meet frequently and go holidaying around the world."

"They divorced some fifteen years back," says Myank adding to their conversation. "Both of them have children from their second and third marriages, but for some reason, even at this stage, they've decided to spend the last good days of their lives travelling the world together."

Anita looks back at the couple. The man is very tall with a hunch and white wavy hair and the woman is slim, much shorter and her face full of thick folds of wrinkles. Together the couple's appearance is charming and gracefully British. They are now looking at an iPad and talking about something on the screen – could be a photograph from one of the islands? Or one from the old days, maybe even a wedding photograph, who knows?

Finding them mooning into each other's eyes while talking in slow, soft voices, Anita says, "They're made for each-other. Made in heaven."

"Your perspective for life changes with age and you realize something about relationships that we don't see in our thirties," says Elissa.

"You may be right. But I don't see Jay and myself like this even after twenty years. I have seen too ugly a face of him. This isn't going to happen with me."

"When things go wrong, you tend to think like that. But circumstances change and could conceivably accommodate an estranged spouse back into your life for company and comfort, if not for romance or sex."

"How do you come by such wise words? Married only for six months, right?"

Myank's head turns towards Elissa abruptly.

"Because I've worked in a marriage counselling centre and have come across couples who remarried their ex-husbands or wives after reaching a certain point in life," says Elissa.

"Did you come across any men who had been sexual perverts or porn addicts?"

"Not yet," says Elissa and starts taking sips from the coke can on the table. Anita sips her drink too. Myank sits toying with his cell phone reading messages and texting.

Soon, Elissa sits pressing her temples with both hands. "I'm not feeling good. At times, I've a problem with motion-sickness."

"Ohh! Have you got a headache?" Anita asks.

"Yeah. Little nauseated. Let me go back to the seat and lie down for a while."

"Oh, sure," Anita says.

She goes back to her seat, followed by Myank.

An announcement declares the ferry's approach to the port of Oia. Anita pinches herself back to the task at hand: that of disembarking with her luggage and boarding a speed ferry to Athens on route to London, where she will have a detailed conversation with Mum and Jay.

She goes to the washroom and joins a small queue for the ladies' toilet. She stands facing a door beside the toilet, the red thick arrow by the door points the way to the emergency assembly area.

When she comes out of the washroom, there is a hullaballoo in the second-class seating area. A few crew members rush over. Anita cranes her neck and sees a few people gathered in a circle around seat number nine – her seat. Something is wrong with the Chinese couple, maybe Elissa, she thinks, and hurries forward to see.

She finds Elissa lying in a pool of vomit and wheezing hard with every breath. Her thin lips, now bereft of lipstick, look thinner wrinkled and dry. Her once-glowing cheeks are pale, and her black tresses are gathered in a messy knot that she might have tied to avoid her hair getting wet with vomit. The crew members make an announcement requesting any doctor on board to come over to help. One of the crew, approaches Elissa with a medicine box and another, who looks senior to the rest, comes to quiz Myank as to whether she had any seafood today, and if this is the first time she's had such an episode.

"Yes, she did. She had squid and mussels."

"Did she have wine as well?"

"Yes, she did."

'Red or white?"

"White"

"Has she had similar attacks before?"

"That I don't know. I'm unable to give this information," says Myank.

The man peers at his face, a question mark hanging over him.

"I've known her only recently," Myank says with a shrug of his shoulders.

"Look, it seems like she has a severe seafood allergy, and we don't have medical support on board. All we can do is give her a couple of injections to stop the vomiting. Once we reach Oia in ten minutes or so, you need to rush her to the hospital. We'll arrange a wheelchair and an ambulance for you."

Now a woman from the crew comes up and shoves a syringe into Elissa's right arm.

"Are you her husband or boyfriend?" she asks.

"I'm neither," says Myank, rubbing the back of his head.

Anita's eyes widen and she intercepts. "W… what! Elissa said you've been married for six months."

Once the words are discharged from her lips, Myank's expression becomes vague and then he looks around. His jaw falls slack.

"No, madam," he says in a firm tone and a full voice. "That's not true. I've only known her for the last five days. She is a travel escort and I found her through a website."

He looks into the faces of the male ferry crew, hoping they will understand.

"What's a travel escort?" asks a faint female voice from within the crowd. Anita looks back and finds the English couple looking at each other with concerned faces.

"A travel escort is a call girl," a voice from amidst the crowd informs.

"Oh god!" says the English lady, clamping a hand to her mouth. The man then holds her by her waist and they leave with slow unsteady yet elegant steps.

Anita's exchange of words with Elissa – all her lies and half truths – now start coming to her, and the world around her is reduced to a blur. A call girl. Someone like that nude blonde with engorged breasts and lips on Jay's computer screen. Myank must be a man like Jay, who quite possibly has a wife and kids somewhere on this globe. And being a man, he is working on his career and his sexual fantasies while his wife is looking after the kids, keeping a home ready for him to come back to, and, probably thinking about him from time to time, in the middle of sweeping the house steps or tightening a sheet.

Myank – the loving companion of Elissa, that young woman with sweet round cheeks in a floral dress who Anita has known for the last six hours – is suddenly a stranger to her in her hour of need. And not only that, but the expression he's now wearing is of regret for having associated with her. There he stands, in a corner by an oval window of the ferry, away from the people crowding round Elissa, his hands folded into each other and hugging his body he stands with his weight on one leg, thoughtfully looking at the approaching port of Oia.

Anita sits down on a random seat. Myank comes to sit beside her. He puts his elbows on the table top and leans his forehead on his hands. "I could make up some kind of a lie to tell you, but I chose to tell the truth," he says. "I live in Cardiff and came to

Athens for work. I met her through an adult website. I'm a lonely man with my family living in Shanghai, and I decided to bring her as an escort, for some company hanging around the islands after my work," he says, his words expressionless but clear.

"But you both are Chinese."

"Yes, but we met through a website. I contacted her from Cardiff to meet me in Athens. I paid heavily..."

They exchange a few more words, and she realizes that all that is bothering him is the thought of wasting the rest of his day on Elissa when in the evening he had planned to meet someone about important work. Throughout the episode, his expression has been that of someone trapped in awkwardness from which he needs to wriggle out, one way or another. Maybe Jay too went through something like this on one of his journeys; or may be something worse, or maybe something very humiliating still.

Elissa's breathing becomes more measured. The wheezing seems to have softened. Anita goes to the front of the deck and looks ahead at Oia port, which has now started coming clearly into sight. The shadow of a hawk crosses her and she looks heavenwards and the sky above starts blazing with golden orange and a solitary hawk soars high, then spirals and glides and circles on his way to a place and in a joy only he knows. The ferry moves past a crowd of people gathered on a hillock to watch a beautiful Greek sunset. Covered by mist and haze, the fireball of a sun fades as it drops to the horizon and appears as a ball of pale vermillion.

Elissa is now lying still on the seat with eyes half open. Her thin lips now all swollen and the eyelids looking thicker and heavier.

The lady who shoved the injection into her cleans her mouth with tissue paper and shifts her into a wheelchair.

Out of an inner need to observe a call girl who masquerades to be someone's wife, or perhaps responding to the voice of her upbringing, to be helpful to a person in need, or, to an adventurous spirit within her wishing to explore other lives, Anita goes to Myank and relieves him of responsibility of Elissa – the responsibility of taking her to an emergency room of a hospital and sit by until she recovers.

As Anita disembarks the vessel with Elissa in a wheelchair, a visibly relieved Myank hands an envelope to Anita: Elissa's ticket from Athens to London, tomorrow at twelve noon.

'If she is okay by then...'

As Anita pushes the wheelchair ahead, her heartbeat hastens at the thought of this innocent-faced Elissa sitting in the chair is a prostitute exposing herself in adult websites.

After collecting her luggage, she gets into an ambulance provided by the ferry's staff, and heads to the nearby hospital. As the ambulance sets off with its siren blaring and revolving red light, cutting through the crowd of thousands at the port, Anita hopes Elissa will be well by the morning after, and she'll be able to see her off at the airport before catching her own flight to London in the afternoon, where she has a lot to sort out in her own life.

The Unbecoming of Anita

People of the locality were telling one another that there was a newcomer drifting in and out of the stalls and stores of the market nearby. They were the people who really had been 'in town', in the sense that they had not moved in recently, and were quite unlikely to move out of the locality or ahead in life. Joydeep had been living in Kailash for about six months now, and was accustomed to its ways. From behind the wide glass windows of the café where he sat for hours on the second floor doing office work on a laptop, he would throw a glance, on and off, at the passersby in the market below. Of late, he too had begun to take an interest in fresh arrivals into the area. He caught sight of a young woman passing along the market lined by make shift stalls and street food vendors; she was mostly clad in a track suit returning from the gym or the nearby park with a long walking track. She had a creamy complexion, was medium built and had a chest as high as the beach beauties of 'Baywatch'. And she had an outstanding arse –the kind of arse most men in their manly side mouthing would say that you could settle a mug of tea on it.

Later he ran into her in the nearby Deer Park where she went for evening walks and at times in the grocery super market. Even in the super market, she was always alone, fiddling with her cell phone, wearing salwar suits or denim pants with her hair loosely tied at the nape of her neck. She always seemed to be in a hurry once she was out of the grocery store or the nearby beauty salon to cross the road to get to the other side of the road, and reach the tall iron gate that lead to a residential enclave. She would disappear across the gate where stood a chowkidar guarding it round the clock, her hands often full of shopping bags. Nobody knew who she was, and yet showed remarkable interest in her movement around the place.

As he never saw a husband or any friends with her, Joydeep assumed she was living all on her own in a nearby apartment. He was about fifty and had two daughters – fourteen and twelve years of age. His family lived miles away in Faridabad where he could afford to buy a home big enough for the four of them, and himself lived in a one room studio apartment in Kailash Colony for ease of transportation to his office located in the heart of the city. He started working quite early in life due to family pressure. And he had been talked into marrying soon after he started working, and the choice of a bride was based on financial reasons. His wife – the daughter of the owner of a renowned Bengali sweet shop chain now looked nearly ten years older than he did, though in reality, she was younger to him by a couple of months. She was a thick woman now, dignified and imposing in silk saris most of the time, and, as she said of herself, was a 'no nonsense person', and called her husband 'Joy' more out of authority than of love. Though he secretly considered her incompetent and dreary, he loved the pecuniary advantage of their marriage, but always disliked being at home. He had first begun his journey of infidelity long ago and he was now constantly unfaithful to her.

Right from his initial days at office, he was never at ease in the company of men, with whom he always maintained nothing more than a working relationship. But he felt quite at home among women, and knew how to behave with them or say just the right things at the right time to put them at ease instantly. There was a mystery in his eyes, an elusive expression and a charming disposition which attracted women ever since his college days. He knew this and was himself attracted to them. Like most men, he generally liked women with a normal body weight paired with reasonably pleasant facial features, a soft voice and feminine ways. The allure of his knack of attracting women had remained dormant in his late twenties and the whole of thirties after his marriage, but soon after he hit his forties it became more prominent than any time before.

As much as he had been enjoying the series of affairs over the last couple of years, he had always known that though every new episode of intimacy added a thrill to the monotony of an ordinary life, it may lead to an extreme complication of his life. Staying away from entangles was what he had been lucky about but he was well aware of the threats that came to him every time he had such an encounter. But every time it so happened that he had so much desire surged up in him that he forgot the possible consequences of the liaison and enjoyed the relationship as a simple romantic association like that of a young college boy. He also believed that loose moral values of a person as accused by the connoisseurs of societal norms was only the creation of their envy for those who had the propensity for this art. And such people would have only gladly transgressed themselves into such enchanting adventures had they known how to set out for it.

One evening, then, while he was snacking at the open air restaurant meters away from the park, the same newcomer lady with a creamy complexion came strolling up and took a seat at a neighboring table. Clad in a track suit, her general demeanor, expressions make-up, hairstyle, all told him that she was back from a jog or a brisk walk in the park, was from a wealthy family, that she was married, and that she was from a small town and was in Delhi for the first time, lonely and probably bored.

The lady was a few yards away from him. The sight of her smooth skin glistening with tiny beads of sweat and her cheeks made rosy by the brisk walk in the park, and her soft lips closing on the straw drinking the strawberry drink from a tall glass did something to him; he felt the titillation of a hundred and one chemicals being released from his brain, and a predatory expression started flitting his face. The hunger again for the wild sensations brought flashing in his mind; the past vignettes of his prized conquests, of long drives to city suburbs, nights in resorts far away from the city came into his mind's eye, and he thought of another brisk affair of lust with a woman who seemed much younger and prettier than all those with who he had a relationship so far, suddenly took possession of his mind very much like many times before in the last couple of years.

Gulping down the bits of the mouthful of the tikka burger in his hands, he slid down on his seat towards where she had been sitting to ask her for a paper napkin from the stack in the napkin holder in front of her on her table.

The lady cast a soft decent glance and handed him the napkin holder.

"I just need one," he said.

"You can keep this on your table. I don't need any," she said, and looked away.

"Okay. Thank you," he said. Soon, to continue holding the thread of a conversation he added, "Do you live around here? In Kailash?"

She nodded.

"How long have you been here?"

She rested her eyes at him for a second before saying, "About ten days."

"And I am dragging out my sixth month here," he said.

She raised her eyebrows with a slight nod and started looking at her cell phone screen scrolling down a page, clicking once here then there. Neither spoke for a few minutes.

"The days pass quickly, and yet life is so dull out here," she said fixing her glance on the screen, not looking directly at his expectant face waiting for words out of her mouth.

"You're saying that you're bored in this bustling city?"

"Yes, bored. Thoroughly. And oh God! The heat, the pollution!"

"I think you may like or dislike this city, but boring? Nah! Boredom, I heard some Babaji say in a Satsang, is nothing but a rage within. An inner rage for desires. It's a desire for desires. So, what I think is, look inwards when bored. Take my words, I'm also speaking from my experience; it's not the city that makes your bored. The heat and pollution is true though," he said and flashed a smile.

She smiled a little. Then they both got busy with their food and the drink and sat in silence like strangers. After a while, they paid their bills separately and simultaneously, and walked out together. Once on the street, they embarked upon a light conversation. They walked towards the tall gate leading to apartments of the locality beyond which she disappeared every day whenever his eyes followed her. They strolled remarking on the spectacular light effects of the pollution fogs around the neon street lights, the glare of lustful looks of men that almost every woman on the Delhi streets come across every day, cries of road rage, and the moon that rode up a fading sky. There was a big bright moon on the sky after the parching hot day. Joydeep told her he was from Kolkata, had a degree in science and worked in a multinational oil company it its Delhi office; that he had at one time trained himself to sing playing on the Spanish guitar, but later in his life he had given up on the idea; that he owned two houses – one in Delhi and one in Mumbai. And from her he learned that she had grown up in Kanpur, but had been married into a traditional Lucknow family – a joint family where lived twelve people under the same roof, where she had been living for two years, that she would stay another month in Delhi, and that perhaps her husband would join her in the apartment at Kailash once his work was over in Chandigarh. She was quite unable to explain whether her husband was the owner of a business, or if he was on the board of the company, and was greatly amused at herself for this. Further, Joydeep learned that her name was Anita Singh.

As he lay down on his bed that night, the meeting with her that day played and replayed again and again in his mind. He remembered her looks, flutter of her eyes, short brisk eye contact while talking and an overall constrain all over her while having a conversation with him – a stranger. It seemed to him that it was only a couple years back that she had been a bride – that too a young bride, and, still in her first youth. It was possible that it was the first time in her life that she found herself alone in a city without her parents or without her husband, and in a situation in which men could eye at her and follow her, and speak to her with their own secret agenda. Her long fingers with manicured nails and dark nail paint, delicate neck lined by a string of mangalsutra with a small pendant that was a cluster of large diamonds, her deep brown eyes, her smooth forehead with a tiny dash of vermillion on a mid parting formed a cloud over his eyes keeping him from falling asleep for a long time, tiring him of the play of his own mind.

A week had passed since the beginning of their acquaintance. It was a windy summer day and outdoor everywhere was all dust and grime; women's *dupattas* blew off them and birds arranged and rearranged themselves on the lines as they chirped hard with the gushes. Joydeep, like any other day, went to the café once back from his office in the late afternoon.

In the evening, he walked to the Lodhi garden where Anita joined in pyjama like pants and a frilly top for a walk. There were a great many people strolling about the walking track and the magnificent architecture of the fifteenth century; some were decked up in ceremonial clothing clicking away photographs against the backdrop of greens, ancient rubbles of tombs, or standing in various poses. And there were some groups of friends or colleagues engrossed in business conversations sitting on the benches. The peculiarities of the Delhi crowd stood out distinctly – the elderly ladies tried to dress very youthfully, the newly married girls tried to look traditional, homely, a bit coy wearing red glass bangles on their wrists.

As they walked on the tracks around the Bara Gumbad, under a magnificent sunset, Anita's eyes scanned the people as if looking for someone, maybe fearing running into some acquaintance. But, she still kept up the talking drawing vague and funny conclusions of her observation of people sitting on the benches. She would throw a sentence here, another there, at times forgetting immediately what it was she had wanted to know and why, and even leaving a few half said sentences hung in the air.

Soon the falling mire of darkness turned faces into blurred maps and a person could no longer be identified from even a distance of a few yards. The wind came back, and the evening cacophony of birds became loud and bizarre. Joydeep and Anita stood on a lonely patch of the carpet grass by the Shisha Gumbad – the tomb with glass engravings on it. They were at the other side of the tomb which was little deserted, away from the walking tracks. He started doing stretching exercises – side stretches, leg stretches, and arm stretches. She stood throwing guarding glances around her. Once done with his stretches, he walked up to her. Both their eyes kept throwing guarding glances all around, and then stabilizing his glances, he concentrated on her face in a steady gaze. She fell silent, and under his gaze she blushed and looked at the rose shrubs and the hedges intently even in that dusk. She avoided glancing at him as if her eye lids grew too heavy to look up at Joydeep anymore.

"It's turned out to be a fine evening, isn't it?" he said.

She nodded her head.

"So what next?" he asked. "We can go for a long drive in my car. What do you say?"

She said nothing.

He looked at her for a while, and then took her in his arms. She remained still with her eyes looking down; he kissed her lips, and then, the softness and dampness of her lips closed round him. He released her soon, and the very next moment he looked around him in alarm – had anyone seen them? That was unlikely in that elusive twilight, he thought.

"Considering the kind of street crimes happening against women around Delhi," he said as he held her hand, "It's better for us to remain safe in the privacy of a home than land in any lone corner of a street for privacy," he said.

She nodded her head shyly.

"After all, you're such a gorgeous woman," he whispered into her ears.

They started walking holding hands for a stretch of the walking track leading to the parking lot where his car, a maroon sedan, was parked.

The stuffy living room of her spacious apartment smelt of a room spray. Joydeep settled on a soft leather sofa as she made a few phone calls and then went to the kitchen and brought him a cup of tea. All this time, listening to her girlish voice talking on the phone, looking at her youthful ways he found her a bit like his own daughter Tina – the elder one who was in high school. He sat thinking how strange his life had turned out to be; full of secrets – secret affairs, dark and mysterious.

This woman Anita had been an even more pleasurable experience. Even when she was clad in layers of clothing, her little reserved ways and her inexperience with infidelity, her thoughts and candid expression regarding this illicit affair as something special, serious and yet sinful, aroused every nerve and cell in his body. She seemed to be constantly in fear of getting discovered with him. Her surreptious looks receiving his kisses, the ringlets of various sizes of her hair brushing against her neck as she spoke or even the simple fall of a strand of her shiny hair onto her bosom aroused him like never before.

"It isn't right, is it?" she said. He stared at her face for some time and rose from his sofa. She sat where she was with a cup of tea in her hands.

"What is not right?" he said once he reached the window overlooking the lane below.

"I don't think, you or any genuine man or woman who knows about this will ever be able to respect me anymore," she said looking at his back and then down with a guilty sulk.

A silence prevailed as he sipped his tea trying to understand what was wrong with her, what was bothering her. His mind ruminated about things that kept coming to him one by one on their own.

Anita, to him, revealed the purity of a naïve woman, but who was yet to see a great deal of life in general to be prudent and tactful in life. He looked around the room – a fully AC luxury apartment it was with fine finishing of walls, expensive wall papers, maple wood floors, door and window frames. The only bulb burning on one corner of the room lit up a few features of her face that reflected a heavy mind or a heavy heart.

"You should know what you want in life," said Joydeep at last. "You have your choices and the choices you make in your life define you. And, accordingly, you eventually get what you want if you're consistent with the choices you make."

"You're right, it's my choice to be good or evil," she said.

"Or stay stuck where you're or set out to find what you enjoy doing."

She immersed herself in a sea of thoughts. Then as she looked up, her eyes filled with sudden gush of tears. "It's terrible," she said.

"Look, you don't need to justify yourself all the time in life."

"How can I justify myself? It isn't just my husband I have deceived, but it's myself. I have been deceiving myself for ever so long. My husband is a good person, but he's so… so much of a man that he doesn't understand women. And he seems to be most comfortable with men especially those with whom he works – his business interests. I don't know what he does at his office, but I know he has some kind of a personality disorder. I was only twenty when I married him, and I found myself thrown into a lonely island. I became so alone with him. I've been wanting something more from marriage. I always believe there must be a different kind of life, a different kind of relationship that makes you feel fulfilled. A different life that gets complete with your association with just one person, and that life is invariably much more than this life I'm living. I wanted to live, I still want to..."

"Are you alone or lonely? There's a difference."

"I'm very ah… l… one," she sighed.

"Hhmm… how did you land up in this Delhi apartment all alone?"

"I have been burning with curiosity about man, about life... my husband travels a lot for work, so this time when he was going to Chandigarh via Delhi, I told him I was sick, and I came here for medical consultation. And then I started going about like one possessed woman."

Joydeep listened to her. Neither her words nor remorse was something he could fathom to the intended depth; it was so unexpected, so out of place.

"I don't understand," he said. "Are you sure you know what it is that you want from life?"

She came close. Their eyes met for a long while. She then leaned forward and pressed her face on his chest. He put a gentle hand on her back.

"I'm not sure I know that. But I don't know what I'm doing now. I'm not a teenager in college; and when I was, I hadn't felt such emotions. What is it that I'm burning with now? Is it a different kind-of-love at a difficult stage of life?"

"These are different depths of love – inner depths and inner needs," he murmured.

He held her closer, fixed his eyes deeper into hers, kissed the terrified expression away from her face, smoothened the folds of stress around her lips, her eyes and gradually she calmed down; and it didn't take very long when she regained her child-like cheerfulness back.

After about an hour or so, they went out to the market that had a deserted look; music of bhangra beats with high bass effect emanated from a parked car. A solitary rickshaw puller cycled by them, honking its rubber honk sleepily to deliver bread and bakery in the neighbourhood colony.

They went to a taxi rank and found one to go to Surajkund to watch a musical rendition that she wanted to see and for which she had two entry passes. Anita said she herself was an accomplished sitarist and was the owner of a music academy in the suburbs of Lucknow city not too far from her home.

He looked at the writings on the envelope containing the entry passes, "Hhmm... Rakesh Singh. Is it your husband's name?"

After the musical was over, they stayed in a hotel room.

Early in the morning, they walked down to the Surajkund lake and sat down on the bank facing the waters. They sat without talking. A few patches of white clouds rested motionless above their heads. A woman sweeper started sweeping the area with a bamboo broom, cleaning the earth around. The rhythmic sound of sweeping and an occasional bird chirping fell in their ears. A temple bell echoed piercing the silence, reminding them of life, of nature, and the natural laws of life. The sun emerged pushing the clouds aside. The sweeper woman at a distance threw her broom down on the ground and folded her hands to the sun God, her eyes closed in sheer sincerity of her prayer. She definitely was praying for salvation from her karmic balance – her good karma or bad karma from her previous births or this birth. The mornings have been like this long before there was any Joydeep or Anita or even the Surajkund or that sweeper woman, and it would go on repeating such mornings, just as indifferently with or without us. And in this continuity of life on the planet lies hidden the equation of our karma that takes us through cycles of birth and rebirth purifying and teaching our souls to attain perfection – the ultimate salvation.

"There's mist on the grass," said Anita, breaking the silence.

"Seems like mist, yes. The sun is up and out and this will soon disappear. Time to go home."

"Office?"

He nodded and they went back to the city.

After this they met every day at noon in the garden, lunching and snacking together in eateries around the park, going for walks, and enjoying a musical, a movie or a play in the nearby theatre. Quite often, she had many questions about their association in an affair followed by a disgruntled look on her delicate face. If they landed up in a patch where there was nobody in sight around them, he would draw her to him and kiss her passionately silencing each and every disgruntled groan within her mouth. These kisses in a public place in broad daylight, Anita's furtive glances and the thrill and fear of getting discovered, gave him the new lease of life that he always looked for. He made love to her with sudden impetuous passion, while she would always wear a hesitant expression with sadness about it.

All this time of their rendezvous around the city, they kept expecting her husband to arrive. But a phone call came in from him when he told his wife that he was having some trouble with his business, that something emergency cropped up and he would be going back to Lucknow directly from Chandigarh and implored her to come home as soon as possible.

Anita made hasty preparations for leaving.

He drove her down to the airport and before she disembarked from the car he looked deep into her eyes. There weren't any tears, but they were mournful and withdrawn.

"If you don't text me, I'll understand," she said. "If you don't call me, I'll understand. And if I forget you, I hope you'll be kind enough to understand," she said it all looking down.

"Give me a last hug, one last kiss. One last look. That's right," said Joydeep as she looked up into his eyes.

"I shall think of you... I definitely will," she said. "But at this point of life, I have realized that some people can stay in your heart but not in your life. Please remember, this parting is forever. In fact, we ought never to have met."

She sighed. He moved her baggage on a trolley up to the entrance gate manned by security personnel, and watched her disappear in the crowd across the gate. So that was an intervention of fate. Destiny had conspired and brought this madness to an end, as quickly as possible. As he drove back to his home where his family lived, he told himself that this had been just one more of the many adventures in his life, and now that it, too, was over, leaving nothing but a memory.

That evening was sultry and dark under a sky with thick grey clouds. The last month had taken him through the peak heat of a Delhi summer. And now was time for the monsoon to arrive. And it seemed the monsoon this year had arrived earlier than usual.

When he got back home, he had his dinner with his wife and children. He tried to play a good husband, a good father and talked to each of them and watched television together for the whole evening until a late dinner and then slept with his wife, holding her in his arms.

The next day also passed by with his family in the Faridabad house; he was busy making a paneer dish for his wife and a spicy chicken for the kids. Around bedtime that night, he searched his office files in his mind and then in the laptop for any pending work. And there was some work pending ever since he had first met Anita in the restaurant by the Deer Park.

"I will go out of the city for a week or so," he told his family over the dinner next day.

"Where are you going?" asked his wife.

"I have some touring to do in a few offices in various cities," he said. "I will start from down south – from Chennai."

"Which cities, papa?" asked his elder daughter.

"Hhmm... Chennai, Bangalore, Mumbai, Kolkata and, and maybe Lucknow," he said.

When he went to Chennai, it was raining already; the air was humid and hot, people moved about the streets with thick black umbrellas in their hands. And on the beaches, the sea was high and roaring. He went to the beach with his laptop slung on his chest and spent his time pacing about the place amidst dispersing coastal crabs. He ate sea fish fries in an open air thatched restaurant on the beach facing the sun set; a sun set that most of the women he had an affair with will call 'spectacular' considering the way the sea waters reflected the golden rays and the landscape around with the extremely tall slanting coconut palms swaying to sea breeze. He sat there for hours. He sat on the rocks that the sea waves kept bashing against. He climbed up the rocks to the dry top to sit meditatively thwarting off the haunting memories. The play and replay of memories of Anita tired him inside out. While in his office doing crucial business, he would go into a spell of swirling thoughts, smiling at his memories with Anita and at times he found a peer or a friend asking him the reason he was smiling or who he was laughing at. At times when a colleague sat down on the empty chair near him to discuss something, he would feel like stirring back into life from sleep.

Anita accompanied him everywhere tiring him of himself. At times while sleeping he could hear her breathing by him, or her giggles would echo from his chest where she lay her head for a long while after love making.

After Chennai, he travelled to the other cities spending all his time at work. He immersed himself in work to keep away from unwanted thoughts and visions. It was pouring in all the cities he travelled to.

He had believed that in a month's time or so, the thoughts of Anita would become nothing but a vague memory like the other women in his life before her. But time flew past and the month was now well over. But Anita was as fresh and clear in his mind as if he had just met her the day before. And his memories of her grew more and more insistent and lingering in his mind while awake and even when deep in his sleep.

It was raining cats and dogs the day he reached Lucknow. He engaged the best suite in the hotel, which had a feathery master bed, colour coordinated interiors, and a flower vase of crystal with vibrant lilies in it. There were a couple of fine oil paintings on the walls, the one over the master bed was a palette of maroon and deep green – a beautiful dame flashing a deep cleavage and deep inviting eyes.

That day happened to be Sunday. So Joydeep had time to go around the city looking for Anita. He had brought the envelope of the entry passes to the musical in Surajkund along with him in his laptop bag. With her address in it, he went over to Gomti Street in a hired taxi and soon located the house where lived Anita. A tall iron gate of white marked the entrance of the sprawling house of an old style that was manned by a guard.

He slowed down the car to look at the doors, windows and the lawn of the house, and any trace of Anita around it. He walked up and down the street, had his breakfast in an eatery in the vicinity of the house. He watched the people around all the while keeping an eye at the house at a distance. An hour later, as he drove past the house in a slow pace, the faint, vague sounds of an Indian classical raga on a string instrument reached his ears. That would be Anita playing a sitar. That was when the front gate opened and a car came out and he decided to follow it. He followed it for some time, but inside the car was someone else – an elder lady and a little girl. Anita's mother in law maybe with a niece of Anita's. He thought of calling her cell phone number. But his mind reasoned against it, after all it would be tactless to embarrass her by calling at this time when her husband might be around her. And a text message might fall into the hands of the husband, and bring about trouble.

He stopped his car on one side of the street and opened his laptop, and searched for classical instrumental music schools in and around that part of the city. He went to each one of those schools, asked a couple of people about her, but there wasn't anyone who knew her.

One whole day passed by.

Early next day, as he went out for another day of searching, he noticed a few hoardings on the roadside with sitars and other musical instruments advertising in enormous letters the mega performance of a certain music school at the local theatre - *The Natraj Theatres.*

From a vague intuition of his strained mind, he thought that it was quite possible that the owner of this performing school was Anita, and in which case she would invariably be there.

The theatre was full. It was a large hall with vintage Islamic interiors – upholstery of green and gold, dangling chandeliers of old style; the crowd in the gallery fidgeted noisily. Then, the curtains went up and the lights dimmed. Joydeep's eyes roamed eagerly over the entrances and each face of the audience in the front rows.

Anita came in. She came in accompanied by a man in a sherwani. Clad in a traditional sari of maroon in silk and chain jhumki earrings, she seated herself in the third row. And when Joydeep's glance fell on her, his heart seemed to stop, and he knew in a flash that this woman seated in a front row of the theatre had filled his whole life in a matter of a few weeks, and was now all that he desired in this life. Even at that late age of fifty, he felt he had fallen in love for the first time in his life. The lights dimmed further.

The light golden light from the projection lights around the stage falling on her smooth skin, threw the unusual beauty of Anita a shade more beautiful –mysteriously so. The man accompanying Anita was a stalky, tough looking man with a mustache, who took the seat beside her. This must be her husband, whom, she had once called a 'man's man'. And there really was something about him – his mustache, and the thin rimmed golden glasses he had been wearing. And his occasional smiles at people greeting him were tight and every bit measured, calculated by every inch.

The husband went out with someone who came over to him and appeared to be someone of his business interest. Joydeep came out to the corridor to check on him and found him settling down into a sofa with three other man discussing things. Joydeep came back to the hall where Anita was left alone in her seat. As the feeble sounds of amateurish sitarists played at the background, Joydeep, who had taken a seat two rows behind them, went up to her at this opportune moment and said in a trembling voice, with a forced smile: "How d'you do?"

The moment her glance met his, she turned pale, and looked at him and around herself in alarm, unable to believe her eyes, squeezing her mobile phone and the tiny white clutch purse in one hand, evidently struggling to overcome a feeling of faintness. They remained where they were for a long while – she sat where she had been sitting, and he stood beside her. As a rendition was over and the musicians were getting ready for the next, the sitars and sarongs sang out as they were tuned, and there was a tense sensation in the atmosphere. Anita grew too conscious of being watched from all the sides of the audience boxes around her at and above her level. Her head seemed to have started spinning. She got up and moved towards the exit nearest to her. He followed her where she was leading him along and across the corridors, up and down stairs; figures flashed by – men in kurtas and ladies in flambouyant anarkalis or salwar kameez suits. She stopped on a dark narrow staircase at the end of a corridor.

"What is this? You frightened the life out of me!" she said, breathing heavily, still stunned. "What made you come? Why did you come? Why?"

"Anita," he said. "But, Anita... Just try to understand... "

She cast him a glance of fear, despise and then, then of love, and then looked at him for some time as if to ascertain herself that it was he, who was standing before her, and in real life. In spite of her words, every nerve and cell of her body appeared to him to have wanted him by her all these days after she had left him in Delhi.

The uttered words were as meaningless as the wrappers of candies in a candy box.

A gush of tears ran down her cheeks. She cried putting a palm on her mouth muffling the sound of weeping. He came forth to hold her in a comfortable embrace.

He let her cry for some time, saying nothing to disturb the silence.

"When I came back from Delhi this time, it was only my body that moved from that place. My mind was left with you. I could think of nothing but you the whole time. I tried to forget but…"

On the landing above them were two youngsters – one was clean shaven with a ponytail and the other with a fine goatee, smoking and looking down at them with keen eyes. But Joydeep did not care, and, drawing Anita towards him, began kissing her face, her hands, her fingers.

"What are you doing Joydeep? What are you doing?" she said trying to hold herself back from him.

"You should know what I am doing and why. You know how have I been looking for you all the while after you had left asking me to forget you?"

"Please leave. Go away from me, please," she implored.

Footfalls of someone ascending the stairs fell on their ears.

"Someone, I think my husband is coming. Joydeep, you must go away now," went on Anita in a whisper drawing her hands off him. "Please let it go now. I promise I'll come to you in Delhi. I have your phone number with me. Now, do not make things any more difficult for me! I'm saying I will come to you in Delhi, I swear!"

As he let go of her hands, she pressed his hand lightly and hurried down the stairs. He kept watching her go. She once looked back at him and he thought her eyes were sad, tired and overall perplexed about life. Joydeep stood where he was for some more time down the staircase where Anita had just disappeared. The two youngsters on the landing kept looking with their heads turned and eyes fixed on her. Joydeep cast a terse glance at them and walked off with heavy steps.

Anita began going to Delhi to see him. Every month or so, she left the town of Lucknow citing false prescriptions and records telling her husband that she was going to consult a specialist on female diseases. Her husband believed her or maybe didn't, but allowed her to go alone considering his tight schedule that wouldn't allow him to accompany her all along. In Delhi she always stayed in a Karol Bag hotel instead of the Kailash apartment of theirs or in Joydeep's studio apartment. Every time she arrived, she would make a call to Joydeep from a public booth or her hotel room and not from her cell phone. And Joydeep who would be eagerly waiting for her, would go to her the moment he received the call, and no one else in Delhi would know anything about it.

A month or two passed by. The rains were over and a chill in the evening air heralded the start of another harsh Delhi winter.

The very first time she came to visit him, she stayed in the Karol Bagh hotel and he went to meet her in a fresh white linen shirt and pair of blue trousers. Carrying a box of dark chocolates that he knew she liked a lot, he went upstairs and knocked softly on the door of her room. Anita opened the door wearing a lahenga of pink and gold that he had gifted her the day after the night they made love for the first time. Exhausted by her journey and by suspense, she appeared pale and looked at him without smiling, but was in his arms almost before he was fairly in the room.

"Have you lost weight?" he asked.

"I don't know."

"Your lightness is unbearable, and it's doing something to me."

They kissed. The kisses were impetuous, prolonged, lingering as if they had not met for years.

"Well, how are you?" he asked again.

"Nothing makes me happier and nothing makes me sadder than you do," she said.

Tears welled in her eyes.

"This is time to be happy and you have tears in your eyes!" he said and sank into a chair lightly slapping his forehead.

She stood leaning on the door leading to the balcony looking outside and down at the street. She now said that she wept because of her bitter consciousness of the sadness of their life; they could only see one another hiding away from people, as if they were blotches in the society – society's black sheep.

"Don't cry," he said in a neutral tone to comfort her as it was only obvious to him that this love of theirs would soon come to an end though he could not say when this end would be. He also thought it was up to them how to make the most of the time together and enjoy it to the fullest. But who would make this woman Anita understand this realty of their present and unchangeable status.

His hair was turning grey, and very fast over the last year or so, he thought catching a glimpse of himself in the mirror of the hotel room as he strode over to her. His shoulders where Anita now put her dainty forehead on was droopy, his tummy underneath the linen shirt he was wearing that day was too loose and fluffy to touch. He pitied her life too, though still warm and exquisite she would probably soon fade and droop like him. What made her love him – an aged man with a sagging body and grey hair? Over the last couple of years, he had met one woman after another, become intimate with each, parted with each, but had never felt love for them. And only now, when he was all grey and wrinkled, had he fallen in love. He never thought this was possible but now, it was there for him to feel and know.

Now after months of intense emotional turmoil making them run to each other, to Lucknow and to Delhi, seemed to them that it was nothing but a cruel game of destiny. They realized it was so much deep and unshakable an emotion that it was not worthwhile to be ashamed of it or there could be no justification, or no argument to prove it wrong or right.

On the fifth of October, as promised, Anita informed of her arrival in the Karol Bagh hotel. Dropping his daughters in his wife's house in Noida where his wife had come to attend a wedding, Joydeep headed to the Karol Bagh destination. He was late by an hour or so and he called the hotel to transfer his call to her room so that he could talk. But every time the receptionist would pick up the call and put him on hold on and then the line would disconnect. It happened a couple of times. Then caught up in traffic that delayed him further, he called her cell phone number. But she didn't pick up the phone – once, twice and then five times. He hit the steering wheel with his fist fearing to have upset her.

When he reached the hotel reception, the receptionist noticed him from a distance and called him to a side.

"You came to meet Anita Singh?"

"Yes."

"She isn't up in her room now."

"Where's she?"

"Don't you know about the incident around noon today?"

"What? Where is she?"

"Wait," the receptionist lady sighed and went to the reception counter and wrote down something on a paper and gave it to him.

"This is the hospital where she is."

"What happened? She fell sick?"

The hotel manager came over to them.

"May I know your name please?"

"Mr Joydeep."

"Your relation to Anita Singh?"

"We're friends. But what happened to her? For God's sake can you tell me that?"

"Mr Joydeep," the lady receptionist said firmly. "There was an incident of rape today. Two men barged into Anita's room and raped her for more than an hour. It was our house keeping boy who suspected something untoward happening inside the room and alarmed us."

Joydeep's legs went limp and he sat down on the floor.

"Mr Joydeep, she's now in the hospital for a medical check-up. We lodged a complaint and the police is with her."

The lady receptionist waved at someone for a glass of water and a waiter brought him a tiny bottle of chilled water. They helped him rise up on his feet and seated him in the sofa chair. A nasty nauseating feeling started moving up and down his tummy, his chest and throat. He looked at the name of the hospital where she was, Good Health hospital. He had been to this hospital before. He rose from his chair heading towards his car to go to the hospital when the manager asked him for his identity card and cell phone number and informed the police about him. After making Joydeep note down his details on a note book and assuring that the cell phone number he had given was indeed his, the hotel manager let Joydeep go.

When in the hospital, the PR executive ushered him to the room where Anita lay surrounded by white curtains from all four sides.

A policeman came over to him and he showed his identity to him and said he was a close friend of hers. Anita he saw was on a bed covered with blankets and was sleeping in peace under heavy sedation.

After meeting the treating doctor and the nurse, Joydeep sat on a chair outside her room, and for all hospital work, he signed the papers as Anita's attendee or guardian.

The whole night he spent sitting on the hospital chair until at four in the morning when the sister informed that she was awake. He walked in the room when Anita's tears started rolling down her cheeks, cheeks paler than ever before, at the sight of him.

"How? How did it happen?" he said. And his hands went up on their own to clutch his head. "How did it happen?"

And they both cried holding each other. The nurses appeared before them asking him to control his emotions. He was then ushered outside to compose himself before meeting her.

The police man too came over for a statement from Anita. She asked them for a moment alone with Joydeep.

When no one was around, Anita whispered to him.

"Joydeep, now that all is ruined, can I still ask you a little favour? Can you save me from the police?"

"Save you from police?"

"I'm very afraid of interacting with the police."

"But now, with such a crime committed, the police is here to help you. And I will make sure the miscreants get punished," he said with a rush of blood in his head. "Tell me what did they look like?"

"I think I've seen the miscreants somewhere before. One was with a goatee beard and the other clean shaven with a ponytail. I think they followed me from Lucknow," her voice went limp and she seemed tired to speak.

After a long pause, she added, "All I want is that you control this situation in some way. I mean I don't want this to reach my husband, my family," she said as a strong overwhelming fear gripped her in a firm panic. She started breathing with her mouth.

"Please don't tell them my name. Please don't tell them my husband's name, or my family…"

She started breathing hard with her mouth wide open and eyes wide open in sheer fear. A tiny muscle on her forehead started twitching. The nurse came over, put an oxygen mask on her and asked him to leave.

Joydeep came out to his chair outside her room. For the first time in his life, he broke into a sob, an inconsolable sob. He went to the washroom. There he cried. And when he was back on that chair outside her room, another policeman strode in to replace the one who had been there all night. He then came to Joydeep.

When the policeman asked him her address, he gave them his address in Kailash, and informed them that Anita had begged him not to file any case.

The policemen looked at each other and went to Anita with the nurse. Once the policemen had left, Joydeep went to Anita who looked at him with the eyes of a helpless child. He put a hand on her. That was to assure that he would be there for her to take care of her and to keep her away from the tangle of police and let her go back to Lucknow safely.

With that, Joydeep had realized that the end of their story happened quite abruptly, unexpectedly with a cursed twist of her life, their life. Unfolding a life of pain and shame. And it was probably the only beginning of their fall.

Not the Sort of Things that Happen Every Day

London, 2018

Dropping Mita at the play area of the school, I waited for the coffee get together in the garden within the premises, scheduled about one hour later. Rather than going back to the lonely apartment, I decided to wait and went forth to watch the assembly proceedings. There were knots of kids of sixth and seventh standards in red-and-white checked shirts and black knickers, and there were three children clinging to one another in shabby casuals and hair, with mouths slack opened.

After a while, once the headmaster was done with his short address and lecture, he asked those three in a clump to come forth, and introduce themselves to the rest of the school. They were recently arrived refugee children from Syria. One of the school teachers made them stand next to the microphone and encouraged them to speak something. I looked at the rest of the spectator kids resting their eyes on those three. Soon one of the three broke into a monologue in a feeble voice. Though he could barely speak English, he did a fair attempt and created a good picture of the war they had witnessed in their country with words, cries and expressions in the sky around them – the gun shots, the firings, the outcries, the people bleeding and shrieking in pain. An occasional interpreter helped the rest of the kids watching understand the gist of things the boy had said.

Feeling the sun on my back in this April morning, I sat down on a side bench to spend some time in that place vibrant with the energies of young people. This felt much better than being in the dingy apartment as I had recently grown too weak to maintain the house all by myself. In fact, I wanted to sell this East London apartment as it was far too big for me to manage, and considered buying a two bedroom for ease of maintenance. But my daughter Maya, who was an engineer in the US wouldn't let me as she had grown up in this house. She had fond memories of this place and said it didn't deserve to be sold off to some stranger. Maya was thirty-five now. Lately, strangely enough, I hadn't known about her marital status. In fact, I've chosen not to ask her about it considering the way young women handled their marriages these days; I mean the ones with a good carrier to fall back upon. Maya had left Mita with me a couple of months back, for a year or so. She paid and arranged for a nanny for three hours every day who would pick Mita up from school at the end of a day, prepare a light snack for her like a sandwich or so, and then take her to a violin class in a nearby music school leaving me with enough time to cook supper.

I now shifted to a stool that lay nearer to the assembled children to see the faces and hear the voices clearer. Those three refugee children, two boys – whose names I now come to know, Adad, Lilith – and a girl Tira, reminded me of my days when I was a little child, which now seemed to me to be another birth altogether, playing with a few Bangladeshi refugees in a village in Northeast India. Those days, I so clearly remember, my parents often left me in their ancestral house when they were busy shifting their business to Calcutta from Guwahati.

It was the early seventies.

I was about ten years old then. That village house was not a house, rather a homestead with a sprawling backyard, a front yard with a flower patch and a barnyard, and what I liked most was that the house had been always bustling with villagers drifting in and out of the doors. Women preparing incessant cups of teas and people sipping tea in glasses as they chatted or did chores or meandered around the yards. So unlike our house in the town where it was only our family –my parents, my brother Dev; my sister Iisha wasn't even born then. I would scamper about the backyard around those tiny white weed flowers dotting the hedges around the house.

Things were different those days. There was a difference in the tones of voices of the people, the way they sounded, the manner of their walking, the way they looked at one another, the clatters of the vehicles in the streets, the kind of food that was cooked, the pace and motion of the air, the ripples of pond waters, the undulations of the beds of hyacinth in the swamps, the darkness inside the thickets of the taro plants and, the swaying of the date palm trees on the lane of the hamlet furlongs away from our house. At times I would scamper away to the nearby temple at the back of which lounged a green pond with a thick lining of moss. In that pond lived a couple of tortoises who looked like upturned saucers floating on the water. I liked to sit at the pond-side below that banyan tree to look at the quiet, introspective creatures existing in peace unaware of the war; of the impending disaster around us.

Those tortoises, grandma said were five hundred years old, meaning they lived for so many hundreds of years in the same waters and under the same patch of sky. They could live for so long, she would say, for all their wise and careful ways about life. I liked that banyan tree under which I would sit to sight my pets – the torts. That tree also was one of a kind; it had roots all over it – wiggling up the trunk or hanging down like serpents of varied sizes. And it was five hundred years old. The two date palm trees, granny said, were about hundred and fifty years old.

Whenever I was there, the tortoises would drift over to the shore, and, there they lay resting quietly, peacefully – the carapace rising and falling with respiration. At other times they would walk about in their lazy pace throwing a glance at me off and on. I'd watch them unwind – stretch their legs and body, and, take long, deep breaths. At times their young ones would come out frolicking. I named the two most mature looking ones who seemed bigger than the rest and who I believed came out to the surface on seeing me on the shore. The biggest of them all I named Ping and the second biggest was Pong. Both of them looked like males, I wasn't sure of that though. Ping was bigger and browner than Pong, his head brownish green and the ridges on his carapace deeper and there were pale streaks around them. Pong was greyish black in places and its head was mottled with numerous yellow, orange and pink spots.

"Anita!" Granny would come calling me for lunch. 'What are you doing here?

"Just watching the torts, granny. They're my pets."

"But you shouldn't be here all alone! That one is an old tree and ghosts inhabit it. They hoist around the pond and if they find such pretty little girl alone they possess her. Haven't I told you before?"

"But, these tortoises are my friends! They will help me if I am in trouble."

"Hhmm.... Don't you think they're too tardy?"

"But granny, they live in that thick shell covering them all over. They want but can't break free from from that. They want to stretch their legs and hands and necks and stomp and scurry about the whole place. One! Two! Three! And you should be able to go running all over the place."

"They appear so wise and sensible. I guess they are too full of wisdom to go for a careless free run and fight with anyone."

"Do you mean, if they did, they would live less?"

"Maybe. You're so concerned about them."

"Poor things, they can't even make a proper sound, forget singing and shouting like us or the animals. What do they do when in trouble?"

"Well I don't know. All I know is that there's something about these quiet,calm creatures which makes them live peacefully and for a long long time."

After lunch that day with grandma, I went to grandpa who was going out to the village for some work. Holding onto his long fingers, I went for a merry-go-round around the village. Grandfather had been one of the most respected persons in the locality. He was thinner than most men and there was something deep about his eyes that gave him a unique presence. An enormous river flowed through the valley. At the fringes of the village adjoining the forest, herds of unicorn rhinos grazed along with the cattle, while the elephant grass swayed blithely with the breeze.

We walked past the highway that ran through the town and by a wide open field near the district court, where only a year back, grandpa said, a huge crowd had gathered when Dalai Lama had arrived there and the villagers welcomed him with a *khada* scarf. I heard my aunts often spoke about those days when village women sat on the ground for hours to stitch up bundles of cotton cloth into clothes and *bakhus* for the Tibetan refugees who had come with the Lama. Grandmother once said, she had even donated the maroon sweater that she had knitted for me to one of the refugee children.

The sooth of the wind had the unicorns sliding down the marshy land into a swamp covered with hyacinth to stay put for hours brooding, and it made me yawn from the depth of my lungs.

The last couple of days of my stay in the village before going to Calcutta to our new home there, I befriended a few children I came across in the streets who were refuges from Bangladesh. I would trot around the paddy fields with one of them, a girl called TukTuk who was a few years older than I was. Farm hands worked in those paddy fields. TukTuk and I would go meet the other children, also refugees from some war in that country who tagged after the female workers and often narrated stories from the streets of Bangladesh. They were Roshul, Sabina and Sakina.

One of those days, as we were at the pond side under the banyan tree, Roshul and another boy came over after a day of sifting through the litter of the nearby town collecting gunny sacks and waste plastic to build their shanties on the river bank. Ping was already out on the bank with a litter of tiny ones around him, or her, may be. I looked at its face, and I could feel its familiar eyes smile in my direction.

Roshul told me that tortoise eggs were so tasty that it was just out-of-the-world, and also good for health but very difficult to procure.

"Have you eaten tortoise eggs?"

"No. I've eaten tortoise meat though."

"Meat? Ya, I too have had tortoise meat once. There are two parts to it – one is just meat and the other is the carapace which softens to a soft leather like consistency on cooking," said Sakina.

"But I can't imagine my pets as my food," I said.

"Let's play with your pets," Roshul went close to Ping. He seemed to look at him and paused for a while before slowly moving towards the water. TukTuk brought a banana from the priest in the nearby temple and gave it to Roshul to feed Ping. Roshul put a small piece of the banana beside Ping, but he lay there. Still. I felt so good to see that Ping didn't accept food from just everyone which made me feel special to him as he would accept everything I fed him. Then we saw Ping move a bit. Then I saw Roshul munching off the rest of the banana as he stared at Ping. And then he came forth to put a thick twig in front of Ping which in a way blocked Ping's way. Ping seemed to get startled at the confrontation. He quietly lay there for some time. Then I saw Roshul throwing a pebble at him.

"What're you doing?" I shouted.

Ping made no move. Then Sakina threw another pebble. And soon she put a fairly big twig near Ping's mouth. Ping retracted his head into the carapace and lay there like an inanimate object.

"Don't trouble him," I said. "Don't trouble him, I say."

"Only playing with your pet, Anita."

Sakina went near and the baby torts resting on the rock at a distance dispersed sensing intrusion and rested under the pebbles in the shallow water hiding away from the intruders.

In a while, Ping started to move its head out and Roshul went to him and touched its top for some time. His eyes threatening and Ping's threatened, horrified.

"Leave him alone, Roshul. I am not going to play with you anymore!" I started moving towards my home.

I went a couple of steps when I heard an outcry. A severe cry. I looked back and found Roshul's right index finger inside the tortoise.

"It's biting his finger!" shouted Sakina throwing a stone hard on Ping. "Leave him. Leave him, you animal," she said. I reached near him for a close look and I saw Roshul getting his hand released but without his index finger!

His hand was bleeding and I ran to grandma to tell her about the incident. To tell her what the mighty Ping had done to the boy – the rowdy boy Roshul.

The clapping of hands in the school assembly kind of woke me up from my trip to sixty years back in time. One of the Syrian refugee boys – Lilith had sung a little Syrian song. Now that the assembly was concluding, the school headmaster came in for a concluding talk and I rose supporting my lower back in my palms.

As none of the mothers were in sight, I presumed there might have been a change of schedule that I probably couldn't follow. I was about to walk out of the gate when I saw a few young women walk in a group and gather in the school yard. They had coffee jugs and containers of snacks in their hand bags; it was a monthly get together of the mothers of the school kids. I dropped in greeting them with a grin. I couldn't wait to sink in my teeth into home-made wafers still warm in the aluminium foil package. I then stuffed myself with two more pancakes from another lady and a cup of coffee from a thermos jug that lay on a garden table. Feeling content, I rose to walk out waving my hands at the other women lost in conversations. I walked up to my home feeling good that the snacks and hot coffee saved me from cooking a breakfast for that day and my old muscles all the effort of preparing a meal and cleaning work thereafter.

And There Hangs the Tale of a Woman

When Dr Dev came to dine in the spring of 1991, a woman came with him to our house, bearing a Barbie doll in a box for me and a pair of eyes that seemed to be in search of something. She was Mrs Amrita, and like Dr Dev who we had known for over a year, she also came from Punjab. Over the dinner, she said that though she was from Punjab, she had grown up in the small town of Sibsagar in the Northeast of India, to which my parents belonged, in the decade of the nineties. Her father had been working in an oil refinery there. Those days, there was severe anarchy in the region – an overall anti-illegal migrants movement, agitation against vote bank politics, unemployed youths, she told us all as well and Dr Dev, her husband who had never been to that place, listened on. A commingling of cultures and tribes, the state of Assam was burning in ethnic clashes. Everybody seemed to be anti-government and every group demanding autonomy and a different state and this was handled with deployment of government forces. Village youngsters were dragged onto streets and shot, elderly men arrested, and women molested. By the end of the summer, three hundred students were said to have died and thousands injured.

Soon after, once the dishes were put into the dishwasher and the table wiped, she and Mum gathered on the master bed in the bedroom for a woman-to-woman talk; I lingered around them. She spoke about her days in Sibsagar on the bank of a historic lake called the Joysagar. I had a faint memory of the lake covered with lotus plant leaves, a couple of lotuses, wild weeds and water birds. I had visited it only once about five years back when I was about eight years old. Mrs Amrita lived in a beautiful bungalow there, she said, and my mum went on to ask which street and whether it was near that kirana shop of Babulal Marwari. She then explained the location with specific details taking Mum through a memory lane to her home in that small town that she seemed to always relish talking about. Both the women went on and on about this family and that, about their friends of childhood hoping to strike up a conversation about someone – a common friend or an acquaintance. In 1999, Mrs Amrita said, her family came across a marriage proposal from Dr Dev's parents, who lived in Punjab and were from her caste. Dr Dev was moving to New Delhi those days to practice in a prestigious corporate hospital as a neurosurgeon. Soon, her parents took her to Punjab for a girl-seeing-occasion when Dr Dev and she met for the first time. Thereafter, in a matter of weeks, her marriage to the doctor was finalized with a small occasion called *roka*. The wedding took place in their ancestral home in Amritsar in presence of her grandparents and all the relatives, who made it sure that each and every wedding ritual as per tradition were followed. After that ceremony of about two dozen rituals, she landed in the apartment on a lane across our house in Delhi, about half a mile away from us.

"Those Shiva temples, hundreds of years old, where as a young girl I used to go every Monday praying for a good groom," Mrs Amrita sighed in nostalgia about the small town of Sibsagar and something more. "They are still fresh in my memory. The fragrance of marigolds and temple flowers in the sanctum sanctorium swath my mind every time I think of those temples."

"Yes, I love the temples there. The architecture's so unique. Very old and mysteriously dark inside," Mum said.

"How far is your home from the Joysagar lake?"

"About an hour's bus ride. My mum and I used to visit the temple quite often," Mum said. "Mother those days would make me fast on Mondays and would take me there to pour a pot of milk on the lingam. I would pray so dearly for a good groom over a grumbling stomach."

"I did the same! And stopped the fasting once I got married."

Both ladies burst into laughter.

"Do you know Mr Kakati's family there?"

"Who?"

"Mr Kakati. He was a police officer and stayed in an official quarter on the lake side meters away from Babulal's *kirana* shop."

"No, I can't remember."

'As I told you I had two good friends – Mita and Ramesh. They were Mr Kakati's children. Mita was in school with me. And her big brother Ramesh was such a handsome guy! He used to come on a motor cycle and was a heart-throb of the teenage lot those days," she said gesturing her hands forward like holding the steering of a motorbike and moving the gears up and down, a vrooming sound escaped her lips in a childish glee followed by a chortle at her own wit.

"Well, I don't know them," my mum said fixing her wide eyes at me, smiling, as I let a tinkle of laughter out. She then looked back at Mrs Amrita trying to assess her personality all over again when I saw a tinge of disappointment in Mrs Amrita's eyes. Mrs Amrita lived in a spacious apartment, about twice as big as ours, at Moti Bagh in Central Delhi. She had two maids coming over to her house to help her cooking and cleaning round the clock. She was rich, and her husband, as she had said, and reiterated for emphasis, was a very busy man and spent most of his time in the hospital he had been attached to, even the evenings. So she often sought some company to go around the place or talk to someone just like that. For that reason, she started coming to our house for an evening chat and to watch the news on any one of the regional NE news channels.

I was twelve years old, and was not surprised that my parents, who maintained a number of northeastern, mostly Assamese acquaintances in the locality, should ask Mrs Amrita to share our meals. Where we lived was a locality with narrow walkways, clogged lanes and brick buildings, situated on the fringes of South Delhi. Most of the regular supermarkets here did not have the usual northeastern cuisine stuff like mangosteen, Indian Olive, elephant apples, the right kind of fish visera for fried rice and many more. In search of compatriots and ethnic flavours, we used to regularly attend all northeastern community functions. Mum went to every kitty party and befriended people with eastern Indian surnames familiar to that part of the world that concerned them.

But their friendship with Dr Dev who joined the university hospital, was a different story, and it was only by chance that they discovered Mrs Amrita's Sibsagar connection.

Mrs Amrita though more sophisticated in her manners and to look at - fairer and slimmer than my mum, wore finer clothes, spoke more or less the same language, told similar kind of jokes, gossiped about other women of the neighbourhood in the same way, laughed at the same puns, and thereby seemed more or less the same to me. After that first dinner, my parents encouraged Mrs Amrita to drop by as frequently as she liked in the evenings when both my parents and I were back home and watching TV over cups of tea, getting ready to cook our supper.

Though my parents had fetched her and Dr Dev in our car the first day that winter, Mrs Amrita later said she preferred to walk from her flat to our home under the trees and along the shrubs on her way. When she entered our house in a puffy perka with hands in her pockets and the hoods over her head, her cheeks were pale in the cold and the tip of her nose was pink with the effects of the chill of the evening air.

Like my parents, Mrs Amrita took off her shoes before entering a room, ate rice every night for supper with her hands mixing pickles into it, chewed fennel seeds with sugar crystals after meals as a digestive, drank no alcohol, and for dessert dipped even the finest cream biscuits into successive cups of tea.

I took to liking her as she often spent time striking a conversation with me in a way that was generous and homely – very north Indian though: she would ask and probe into my school activities and test my knowledge of vocabulary – first of English and then Hindi. She would pick up the globe on my study table and her finger trailed across China, the Marginal sea of the Pacific, the USA, Atlantic, through Europe, the Mediterranean, the Middle East, and finally to the diamond shaped Indian subcontinent. She would circle the places where my parents' were from. Assam was signified by a one horned rhino on the map.

The next weekend evening, Mrs Amrita arrived as usual, at half past six. Though by now they were good friends, upon first greeting each other, every day she and my mum maintained the habit of hugging each other, and to my father would offer an elegant folding of hands in a namaste with a broad smile her shiny red lipstick layered lips stretching over her white teeth.

"Come in, Mrs Amrita. Tania, offer auntie a glass of water please," said father. "How's Dr Dev? Haven't heard from him for a long time."

She stepped into the foyer, impeccably suited and scarved, with a georgette full-sized Punjabi *dupatta* sprinkled all over her chest. Each evening she appeared in ensembles of shocking pinks, creams, and golds. She was a compact woman with feet firmly planted on the ground, and maintaining an efficient posture – erect and chest high very much like a south Indian actress would do. A braid of her thick black tuft of hair rested on her back fell onto her buttocks, or on her front over one of her shoulders and down by the side of one of her enormous breasts, over the glitters of the dupatta. She had thickly lashed eyes layered with black mascara and shaded with a trace of silvery or coppery eye shadow, a generous growth of eye brows, and a mole in the very center of her left cheek. At times, on her head she wore a rich clip ornated with kundan work, secured by bobby pins from below.

We returned to the kitchen after the vocabulary test, where my mother was draining a pot of boiled rice into a colander as she liked to drain away some starch from the grains so as to make it lighter and keep the lipid levels checked considering her borderline diabetes.

"There's a documentary in the North East regional channel today about a great mishap in Assam. You remember, in the Nagaon district where thousands of immigrants from Bangladesh were slain," my father said.

"Yes, I know. What time is it?"

"Ten in the evening."

Mrs Amrita handed me a pouch of hot sweets, for it was my job to serve them to everyone in plates. She then removed her pump shoes and lined them against the baseboard; a layer of mud clung to the shoes, the result of walking a mile through the walkways from her flat to ours. She then followed my parents to the living room as her silver anklets clinked with every step where the television was tuned to the NE channel.

Samosas with coriander and tamarind chutney were laid out in our kitchen bought from the restaurant Mum always passed by while going to work. Mrs Amrita took a bite.

"One can only hope," she said, holding the samosa in a certain angle against her mouth, about to take a second bite, "that such a mishap doesn't repeat as I often get to hear of ethnic skirmishes between the tribals and Muslims even these days."

She then reached for her purse and gave me a small plastic heart filled with éclairs.

"Really, Mrs Amrita," my mother protested. "Please don't spoil her. She has two caries in her teeth and is also putting on weight. "

"Okay. In that case–" she said looking at me attentively.

I was charmed by the presence of Mrs Amrita's flouncy yet flamboyant presence, and flattered by the theatricality of her attentions. Yet was unsettled by the superb ease with which the words flew out of her lips, which made me feel, for an instant, like a grown-up lady of high intellect sitting in a gathering in a house.

For the documentary, another couple from Northeast India who had recently moved in Delhi came over to join us. As the husband of the new couple joined my father and started conversing in a loud voice about Indian politics, the wife stayed quiet and sat through toying with the edge of her sari and her cell phone.

That night, like many nights before, we did not eat at the dining table, but sat outside in the small balcony with potted plants around it. We sat on the cane sofa in a huddle, without conversing, our plates perched on the edges of our knees. From the kitchen my mother with the helping hands of the two ladies, brought forth the succession of dishes: lentils with fried onions, green beans with coconut, fish cooked with raisins in a yogurt sauce. I followed with the water glasses, and the plate of sliced onions, lemon wedges, and green chillis, bought during one of our bi-monthly trips to the super market, which the grown-ups liked to bite with every mouthful of rice. Before eating, Mrs Amrita always took out a flashy watch of white metal, which she kept in her purse, and which she said was a gift from Mita, Mr Kakati's daughter, the school friend from Sibsagar. She held it briefly to one of her ears heavy with gold danglers and with a peculiar look on her face, she said that she liked to have that heavy thing removed from her small wrist for its weight and put on a folded paper napkin on the table to save it from wetness, during all her meals.

I studied her with extra care. I decided that besides that snake-like braid that slithered on her back as she walked, this peculiar look that imbued her personality was one of those things that made her different from the rest of the women. When I took the watch on the folded napkin in my hands that night, as she helped mum arrange the sofa table with bowls of curries, an uneasiness possessed me at the sight of the sensual design of the watch which was a couple kissing lip-to-lip on one end of the oval dial while their fingers entwined on the other end of the dial over a heart shape. The cheap looking watch with areas of unevenness on its surface and a prominent 'Made in China' in the inner side, made me feel something which gave me a peculiar tickle in my chest and I felt for the first time in my life. Life for Mrs Amrita, I realized, was being lived in the memory of someone in another land first, than with her husband in this city.

Her lives, her goals and her actions, I now knew were only a reflection of what had already happened there. A lagging echo of where she once belonged.

At ten, which was when the documentary began on the television, my father raised the curtains over the door so that we could see the screen from the balcony and raised the volume. Usually I occupied myself with a book during such political television viewing, but that night I found myself engrossed on the happenings on the screen. I saw dead bodies in thousands lying on the ground that seemed to be a sea beach, but later I came to know it was the bank of a massive river that originated in China and flew through that part of India. Blood drenched machetes, knives and bows and arrows lay all over the place and forests of unfamiliar trees into which hundreds of a certain group or clan had fled, seeking safety. I saw boats with fan-shaped sails floating on river waters, poky huts made of coconut palms with yards wet with pools of blood and agitated tribal men and bearded men in pallid lungis pace around the streets and school premises.

I turned to look at Mrs Amrita; the images flashed in miniature across her wide kohl lined eyes. During the commercial my mother went to the kitchen to get more rice, and my father and the other gentleman guest deplored the policies of Indira Gandhi, the then prime minister of India. They discussed intrigues I did not know, a catastrophe I could not comprehend.

I sat stealing glances at Mrs Amrita, sitting beside me, calmly creating a well in her rice to make room for a second helping of lentils and smiling at me now and then. She was somewhat a notion of a woman in my mind growing up curious about the human bonding and the intriguing feeling called love between a boy and a girl. I wondered if that kissing watch was a gift from Ramesh – the handsome guy in the neighbourhood where she grew up in. I wondered why she was so gorgeously dressed coming to view a documentary about some grave blood shedding incident years back. Was it in preparation to come face to face with Mita or Ramesh – her long lost love? I wondered, too, what would happen if suddenly the handsome Ramesh was to appear on television riding on a motorbike, smiling and waving and blowing kisses to Mrs Amrita.

I imagined how relieved she would be. And she would abandon Dr Dev and run into his arms in that very instant out of sheer love. But this never happened.

At the end of it, my mum, Mrs Amrita and the newcomer lady went to sit in my parents' master bed. As my mum went to serve the tray of fennel seeds to the guests, I heard Mrs Amrita asking that woman about the Shiva temple in Sibsagar where she used to go for her Monday puja. That woman seemed to know each and every anatomy of that town as Mrs Amrita did. And then she asked about Mr Kakati and finally about Ramesh, as I had been expecting her to. The name Ramesh was spoken with a certain lightness and fondness that nothing else could ooze out of her eyes, and I could somehow identify it with the yearnings in the eyes of the lovers in romantic movies like *Love Story* of Hollywood as well as Bollywood and also the ones in the recently viewed movie *I Hate Love Story*.

"Mita? Mitali Kakati? Yes, I know her," the lady said.

"Do you?" Mrs. Amrita sprang up on the bed. "Where is she now? And do you know the brother Ramesh?"

"As far as I know, Mita married someone in Kolkata and now stays there."

"And Ramesh?"

"He joined the Airforce. But–"

Just then Mum walked in.

"But what? Is he married now?"

"Yes, he got married. But–"

"Who got married?" Mum intercepted.

"There's a man called Ramesh and the poor guy married and all, and also was doing well in his career in Airforce. Was a very charming boy, but it seems the aircraft he was flying a Mig 27 disappeared in the forests of West Bengal somewhere bordering Nepal."

"Oh my God!"

"A… are we speaking about the same Ramesh? Mr Kakati's son? The police officer?" "I don't know whether his father was a police officer," the woman said.

"And what happened to the poor wife? Had he any children?" Mum asked.

"Luckily no children. Again since the Airforce hasn't recovered a dead body or the aircraft yet, they haven't declared him dead. So the wife is living a life of half a widow over the last seven years," the woman said with genuine concern in her voice.

My mum tsk tsked her tongue and steered the conversation to the plight of the half widowed wife.

In an effort to banish the gory image I saw that night, I looked around my room at the canopied bed with matching curtains with polka dots, at the framed water colour paintings I had made with the help of the art teacher at school mounted on pink and white papered walls, at the penciled inscriptions by the closet door where my father recorded my height on each of my birthdays, and at the musical danglers on my window. I pulled the hanging hand of the musical dangler and soft music started to flow. I tried to concentrate on that, ignoring the faint sounds of Mrs Amrita crying inside the toilet of my room and coming out of it faking a smile.

But the more I tried to distract myself, the more I began to convince myself that Mrs. Amrita's old friend in all likelihood was dead.

That night I tried not to think about Mrs Amrita – her kissing watch, her connection to the unruly, sweltering world we had viewed a few hours ago in our living room. And yet for several moments that was all I could think about. My stomach tightened as I worried whether her old friend Ramesh was now dead or living a life as a hostage in any of the neighbouring enemy countries around India – in a jail tortured and starved and sodomised (whatever that meant).

Eventually I went to the small Ganesha statue on my study table and I prayed that Mrs Amrita's friend was safe and sound, and if not, she should get stronger and accept the reality and stop searching for her old love. She should live as normally as my mum did. I had never prayed for anything before, had never been taught or told to. But I decided, given the circumstances, that it was something I should do.

The next day at school, no one talked about the mishap killing thousands of migrants in that part of the world that was followed so faithfully in my living room. We continued to study the Industrial Revolution, and learned about the injustices of taxation without representation, and memorized passages from the Declaration of Independence. During recess the boys would divide in two groups, chasing each other wildly around the swings and seesaws.

The next day, after the television was switched off, and the dishes washed and dried, they joked, and told stories, and dipped biscuits in their tea. When they tired of discussing political matters they discussed, instead, the progress of Mrs Amrita's oil paintings and the peculiar eating habits of my mother's north Indian coworkers. Eventually I was sent upstairs to do my homework, but through the carpet I heard them as they drank more tea, and listened to cassettes of Bhupen Hazarika. They played cards on the coffee table, laughing and arguing long into the night about the spellings of English words. I wanted to join them, I wanted, above all, to console Mrs Amrita somehow.

They played cards until the ten o'clock news, and then, sometime around midnight, Mrs Amrita left our place when I had already drifted off to sleep. Those nights, as I drifted off to sleep I would hear my parents along with a friend or two, who dropped in while passing through that part of the city where we lived, to discuss their anticipation of the birth of a new state in the Northeast of India.

Mira, my friend from neighbourhood dropped in one day dressed in a stylish off shoulder dress picked up from the export reject shops of Sarojini market. I had come to see her off at the gate. I found Mrs Amrita at the end of the driveway her clothes shabby, hair dishevelled and kohl spread far below the eyes. She waved at me and then walked into our house.

"Why that woman is looking like a ghost? Is she on her way to act in some play?"

"She's sad. Her boyfriend is missing."

As soon as I said it, I wished I had not. I felt that my saying it made it true, that Mrs Amrita's friend really was missing, and that she would never see him again.

"You mean he was kidnapped?" Mira continued. "From a park or something?"

"I didn't mean that. He lives in a remote part of the country, and she hasn't seen him once she parted with him.And now somebody told her that he is no more."

Later that evening, in the living room, Mrs Amrita, my father, and mother were sitting side by side on the sofa. The television was turned off, and Mrs Amrita had her head in her hands.

What I remember is that after that day, my father no longer asked guests to spend time with them watching the news or any movie with them. Mrs Amrita stopped bringing me candy, and that my mother refused to serve fancy meals to the visiting guests. I remember some nights helping my mother spread a sheet and blankets on the couch so that Mrs Amrita could sleep there, high-pitched voices hollering in the middle of the night on a telephone, and my mum speaking to someone in urgent tones. Most of all I remember was that there was some sort of silence, fear or anticipation in the air those days.

From all the haphazard clues that I had received from around me all I could make out was Dr Dev discovered a registered letter that she had written to Ramesh about a month back using our mailing address which had returned, not finding the concerned person to deliver. Later, father handed over that letter to Dr Dev without knowing the possible consequences of it. I kept wondering what was it that she must have written to create such havoc in Dr Dev and destroy her marriage to him. Was it what you call a love poem? Or a love letter that owned such immense powers?

In November, Mrs Amrita flew back to her home in Punjab, to discover what was left for her in her father's home after her separation with Dr Dev. My father drove her to the airport one afternoon while I was at school. For a long time we did not hear from her. Our evenings went on as usual, with dinners in front of the news. The only difference was that Mrs Amrita was not there to accompany us. According to reports Assam was still burning in conflicts and clashes under a slew of student leaders and other local leaders and various militant factions. Countless refugees from

Bangladesh shooed away to deserted river banks as the problem of unemployed youth rose further.

A few months later, we received a card from Mrs Amrita commemorating the Assamese new year Bihu, along with a short letter about her life in her mother's house.

Then, finally, about a year later, she wrote to us a letter in a red envelop with golden imprints. She was reunited, she wrote, with her friend – not that old friend from Assam but someone from nearby city of Chandigarh who she had met on her way back from Delhi to Chandigarh. She had shared her story of separation with Ramesh and separation with Dr Dev with him. All were well, she wrote, her new friend was a handsome man who looked a bit like Ramesh and worked in the Indian Airforce. At the end of the letter she thanked us for our hospitality, adding that those words were not adequate to express her gratitude. And she invited us to the upcoming wedding ceremony in a couple of months in a hotel in Punjab.

Probably to celebrate the good news my mother prepared a special dinner that evening, and over the dinner I felt Mrs Amrita's absence around the house and asked my parents about her visiting us.

"She had no reason to return to us," my mum replied to my repeated questions and father told me that we would never see her again in our lives.

The Roots Within (Redux)

Molai forests, 2015

With my groin pressed hard on the sharp edge of a plank of the platform set on a tall tree, as I shoot a film in the wilderness, my mind keeps drifting away to my next mission that starts the morning after. A string of thoughts jumble my mind even when I see the animal walk in the frame of the camera and stand right on the cross-hairs. Ronnie is all excited as we set our eyes on the clouded leopard in a tawny colored coat with spots and patterns on it that lingers there. After about two minutes or so, the animal darts away into the forest. The rays from the sun at the horizon glints off a corrugated branch of the tree, and we get down with the help of lineman's belts wrapped around our bodies. We go back to the jeep and drive off to the State Forest Department bungalow in the thick of this sub Himalayan rainforest known not only for the flora and fauna, but also for the terrorist guerrillas hiding away from government forces.

At sun up we set out for the village. Parking the jeep by the highway under the shade of a banyan tree, we walk down to the alley that meanders ahead forking and re-forking until it comes to a ribbon like width.

"I'm afraid we're not going to get kidnapped for ransom or something," says Ronnie.

"Hmm... Please cover your blonde hair under the cap," I say. "And talk less around strangers. Your accent, you know."

Spotting a passerby with a stack of hay on the back of his bicycle making his way ahead through the path, I yell, "Hey! Where's Dibakar's house?"

He points towards a thatched house amidst a scatter of areca palms. Ronnie cocks his camera in that direction and clicks the rutted laterite lined by purple-and-green taro plants and giant ferns leading to the house, then a couple of clicks of the cyclist with a woven headgear, and then, he's about to follow the string of geese on their way to a pond.

We reach the bamboo gate of the house.

"Mr Dibakar?" I shout several times.

With flanking thickets of plantain groves and a fence of coconut palm leaves skirting it, the house and its precinct is serene; the calls of wood peckers on the trees punctuate the silence that soaks the place. The courtyard is neat with the rainbow patterns of a broom on it. Ronnie strikes one of the bamboo poles of the gate with his metal key ring in the shape of a nude woman. Knock Knock Knock. A girl appears, and I tell her that we're film makers from London and want to meet Dibakar regarding a story.

"Please come in," says she.

We walk in and stand in the courtyard.

"What's your name?"

"Louni," she says looking down and away as I try to hold her glance.

"Lovely place. Green valley, clean air," I say.

Ronnie rolls his eyes.

"Uhmm... would you like some tea?" a feeble voice falls on our ears.

I let my eyes rest on her face – a triangular face, smooth wheatish complexion with a tiny black dot in between her brows; thick black hair in a braid falling on to her taut buttocks.

"Sure, I would like some," Ronnie says and slumps his shooting tool bag on the earth, wipes the beads of sweat off his forehead when a man in a dhoti wrap and a shabby tee walks in. He is Dibakar. He has a tuft of grizzly hair on one side of his head that he combs spreading it to cover all his head. His body is even lankier than mine and height about six feet – almost as tall as me. I press my hands together in a 'namaste' and introduce ourselves. Louni disappears behind the curtains.

We settle on the cane chairs in the yard feeling Dibakar's gaze sizing us up. His English isn't all that bad but has a quaint accent.

"You boys had *luns*?"

Ronnie doesn't follow most of what Dibakar says and I'm sure he is hungry, as he always is when we're out for field work. 'I think tea is just fine,' I say. 'Louni just said she's getting it.'

"Okay then. Now tell me."

"It's a charming place, lush greens, free of pollution," I start my opening gambit.

"For you it's a *–ah*rming place. Exotic life. Good place for holidays and adventure, isn't it? But we've no –oice. This is the only land for us," he says.

Ronnie and I nod our heads.

"So Renu told you about me," he says. "How's she?"

"After a lifetime in England Mum still misses this place."

"I thought people leave behind their memories when they go away to big cities," Dibakar says.

"Not easy. Growning up in a land other than that of my parents." Even I have an inner urge to see and feel my roots. That is one reason why I'm here today. In my London office, I always try to take up the India based assignments."

"Hhmm... And, how's your work going?" he asks.

"We're almost done with the shooting part. Have interviewed a few local people," I say. "Besides the documentary, I'm generally curios about this land. So, Mum had directed me to you for a story or two about the people of this place and that's why she wrote to you."

Louni comes in with a palm size earthen hookah with burning tobacco in it, and hands it over to Dibakar who seemed to beweighing and balancing my words with a keen face, probably trying to fathom my eagerness about knowing the place. Ronnie asks him about the history of this place and as Dibakar starts telling him, about the Tai Ahom kings. Ronnie switches the audio recorder on like any other interview. The Ahom kings, he said, came down from Mong Mao, China and ruled this land for six hundred years until the British took over.

After about half an hour of the chit chat, Louni refills his hookah. Ronnie switches his recorder off. I sit beside Dibakar to show him a sheaf of paper – my collection of old newspapers of the seventies and early eighties for another short film idea brewing in my mind.

They're photographs of girls in handspun and boys in bell bottomed pants and side burns screaming slogans on the streets.

"As I know, you were a prominent student leader during this period of the students' agitation."

He looks at the image of the girl bearing a banner standing in an endless rally of school students. "She's Renu – your mother."

"I know that," I say. "And this girl standing beside her?"

"She's Anamika," he says.

"Mum mentions her whenever she speaks about her early days in this land."

"Yes, they were close friends. I remember seeing them together on their way to school and generally around the hamlet."

"Uhm... Anamika I hear was very beautiful!" I say looking at the picture.

His eyes glimmer a little at this abrupt turn of my questions, and then, withholding each and every expression he looks at me plainly.

"Yes," he says, "very pretty she was."

"Mum said there's a story around her. Will you tell me? Please?" I say sounding like a teenager.

"It's not connected to your work," he says in a tone that sounds more like a rebuke.

"It's connected actually."

"I don't know how."

"Ana, as I learned from my mum faced the harshest consequence of those turbulent times."

He sighs after a silence of a few seconds.

"It was thirty-five years back. I was in my final year of graduation that year, and had got elected as a student leader. That meant managing a sea of students from the surrounding areas to protest against the ruling government's vote bank politics. The processions snaked through these lanes," he says pointing at the alleyway in the front. "Students rallied to the district head quarters, and, most of our rallies ended with a mass arrest when police would prod thousands of students into vans and shuttle them around the jails looking for space."

Sun rays filter through the tall thicket of bamboo grove across from us beyond the bamboo gate and the day around us in the courtyard starts to open up. Old days come alive in the manner of a montage of a motion picture as I listened on.

"Petite Ana in a crisp cotton sari, hair tied in red ribbons with a satchel on her shoulders and a floral umbrella in her hands joined Renu to stand in the rows of the procession."

Louni brings tea and biscuits on a tray and puts it on the table in front of us.

"I've been playing on my mobile," Ronnie says restless, and bored as we sip our teas.

"I'll be back in a minute," Dibakar says and walks inside the house.

"I know you don't understand. I'll explain to you later," I say.

"I heard so much about great Indian hospitality and all. That they treat guests like gods."

"Aren't you being treated well?"

"Americans will offer more than this if you'd lined up a visit for months."

"Come on! What did you expect?"

"Something to eat."

"Beef steaks?"

"Oh! Did you tell that village *hottie* who served tea that we already had our lunch and were full up to our throats or stuff like that while mooning into her eyes?"

"Her name is Louni."

"Whatever!"

"I spoke to her. No flirting. No mooning. She's different from the skanky ones you meet in night clubs. She's pristine!"

"You mean a virgin?"

"You're crazy!"

"By the way, is she the type you would want to marry?"

"Who's talking about marriage?" I say. "But yes, why not? A girl like her will make a great wife and mother."

"I know your Indian double standards!"

"You're going nuts! Only some food will set you straight."

When Dibakar comes over, I helplessly reveal that we're hungry.

"What do you want, omlette or chicken?" he asks Ronnie.

"Whatever is available quickly."

He goes in and, in a while, comes out with a giant omlette. That's four geese eggs.

"I guess you didn't like the tea," Dibakar asks Ronnie.

He shrugs, "It's okay. Something, a drink it is."

Dibakar goes in again and returns with a calabash.

"Most important local custom," he laughs. "Home brewed local liquor that is. We three have a glassful each."

That's when we see a tusker on the lane fronting the house. A young *mahout* in a loin cloth prods the animal ahead. From the rapid and weird rhythm of the tusker and its head movements, it seems wild, yet to be domesticated. Ronnie walks past the bamboo gate as the animal stops to eat plantain leaves by a shrubbery. He strikes up a conversation with the village youngsters. I have a look at the lane fronting the house that forks one more time as it meanders ahead inside the village. My mind conjured up a picture of Dibakar, Renu and Ana leading a procession of thousands of students through that path; voices of young students shouting slogans wafting the air.

I come back to Dibakar in the yard who had been sitting with a flood of recollection of his early days fresh on his face.

I lift the tray that Louni brought the cups in and is lying bare on the table as the fine weaving in it is quite exquisite to my mind. "This is such fine work!" I say. "This kind of bamboo woven stuff is so typical of this region."

"That's woven with Birina weed," Dibakar says. "You can weave very fine with this weed. People even weave out earrings."

"Oh really?"

"Rings of Birina has a romantic connotation in our villages. Lovers are known to use it to weave out engagement rings even before it is time to declare their love to the world and before they have enough earnings to replace that with a gold ring."

"That's romantic!'"

"Even I'd woven such a ring once in my life," he says.

"For the beautiful Ana?" I say.

He nods his head.

"That afternoon is still alive in me. The silk-cotton tree in front of her house was swaying with the breeze. I stood on the alley, meters away from her house waiting for her to show up at the gate. When she popped out of the door to collect the laundry on the line that the wind scattered on the grass. I waved my hands to catch her glance. The moment she caught my sight, I gestured at her with my hand to come over, and, in a few minutes we were together on the alley walking up to the deserted causeway; that was our usual meeting place. That was the most surreal afternoon of my life; I saw the seed pods on the cotton trees around us swirl in the wind and release cotton threads in the air that looked like white confetti. Then, blinding her eyes with one of my hands, I put the ring that I had woven for her on her left ring finger," he sighs. "She was so overwhelmed to see the ring."

"Then?"

"Then, just two days after that, I had to go away. I'd to flee from this place," he says. "Thereafter is a sad story, my boy. Come, I'll take you to Ana's mother. You want to meet her?"

"Okay," I say.

"She's very old now but her memories of those days are still poignant, picture perfect. You okay to walk up to her house?" he says.

Just then Ronnie walks in.

"I had a nice stroll around the village," he says.

"You liked it?" Dibakar asks Ronnie putting a loving hand on one of his shoulders. "You're the first white man with golden hair I've got a chance to speak to, and that too, right in my courtyard."

We set out for Ana's house. After a walk on the maze of ribbon-like alleyways, we reach a house with a corrugated tinned roof, walled off on all sides by a bamboo barrier. The sight of the house makes my heart hammer. My palms get sweaty. My mind conjures up a picture of a young girl prancing about those alleys; I can almost hear the pattering of her feet on the earth. Then I see a red cotton tree on the alley standing by the gate to the house.

"Is that the tree you were talking about?"

"Yes. It's the same tree," Dibakar says.

We stand right at the gate of the house.

"She should be in, but let me check out," he says and goes in the house as we wait there. Dusk is immersing the valley. 'V's of flying geese formed patterns on the sky and we watch the flights with our heads upwards. I also see a young girl in a flowing sari standing on one of those knolls in the field across the alley and looking up at the flying birds.

"Migratory birds," he says. "Must be from Siberia."

Dibakar comes over and ushers us into the homestead in the shape of two 'L's with a quadrangle in between. A dark basil plant stands in pride of place in a mound of earth at the middle of the quadrangle. An old lady comes over in a handspun of oyster white along with a man in a white kurta and dhoti, a thumbprint of white sandalwood paste on his forehead and a long pony tail of grizzled hair. But for that hunch on her back, the slight old woman is almost as tall as Dibakar, all her hair white and tied in a small round bun at the lower back of her head and her sprightly eyes are the salience of her persona. With a slight waggle of her head, she walks up to the edge of a verandah and sits under the eaves of the house, her feet bare and a hand fan of palm leaves in her hands. A few children peep at us from under the curtains.

"Can you hear me?" Dibakar speaks aloud into one of her ears as we sit on the offered bamboo stools.

The old lady nods.

"He is the one I told you about – Renu's son," he says putting a hand on my shoulder as I sat next to him. "They're making a film on us, on this place. And for that they're looking for our stories. I told them, about Anamika in the eighties."

Her eyes narrow a little as a jumble of deep crow feet wrinkles appear around the corners of her eyes, as she looks up at me. Dibakar starts steering the conversation.

"After the state election fraud of 1983, when president's rule followed, the military marched in the village alleys," Dibakar says. This sparks a little conversation between Dibakar and the ponytail man.

The old lady hears them intently, nods her head a couple of times. "Army sleuths in the villages made the lives of the youngsters of those days miserable," Dibakar adds. "Government forces took us into custody on every pretext and the physical and mental torment drew on for days and weeks. So, I fled to a nearby town. I couldn't even meet Ana the day I had left."

Following Dibakar's words as much as she could, the old lady now looks at the situation around her with some new found interest.

"When Dibakar went away Ana was in a sad mood," she says looking into my eyes. Dibakar encourages her to speak and her voice crackles with age and her memories of a daughter as she spoke.

"After the household chores those days, I found her stuck on that window," she says pointing at a window at the far end of the elongated house facing sprawling paddy fields at the back. My glance scurries away to the window and my mind pictures Ana looking out of the window resting her head on one of the iron railing of it. "She would write letters to him every day. We used to sleep on the same cot, and I saw her sleeping a very light sleep. She would wake up to owls' cries and even to the crunching sounds of the bats landing on the litchi tree." My eyes rove around the courtyard to spot the litchi tree she just mentioned.

"Then?"

"Then, one afternoon, like most of our autumn afternoons, I had been spinning cotton yarn right in this quadrangle, when, I heard a commotion in those lanes," she says pointing towards the alleyways in front of her house. "A few soldiers had a skirmish with village boys. I went out to find out what the percussion of canes and leather boots had been. That was when, finding the stool next to the spin empty, Ana came to take over the spin where I had left it. Later, all I heard was rush of feet around the house and when I went in I found Ana in the barnyard."

"How many of them did you see rushing out?" I ask.

"Two of them," she says again. "Two ran out of the house to join a few others on the street."

"And?"

"When she opened her eyes on the hospital bed, Dibakar's mum and I were sitting by her. On gaining consciousness, the poor girl lost consciousness once she remembered the sequence of events."

The old lady stops.

We sit in silence under the light of a full moon and a distant bulb hanging in the veranda of the house. A few insects flit on the bulb making it pendulate in the palpable heaviness of the air that night. A sharp wail of a child from inside the house pierces through the thick air.

A tray with cups of tea arrives. I pick up one and sit thinking about that situation thirty-five years back, right here, in front of this old lady. Once everyone else finished with tea, a lady proffers a plate with raw areca nuts and betel leaves. As the pungent sap of the leaves spread on my throat I ask Dibakar, "What happened after the rape? What did you do?"

"I didn't meet her after that," he says. And then changing the note he adds, "We can now go back to my house. It's already midnight."

We walk following Dibakar on the lanes now bathed in a silvery glow of moon light. That night, we spend in Dibakar's house. We don't speak. I can't eat my dinner either.

At the crack of dawn, Dibakar gives us some ash from the kitchen hearth to rub on our teeth. As I walk out to the yard, I find the morning sky overcast. Louni offers our breakfast of roasted rice powder, jaggery and milk. Ronnie and Dibakar strike up a conversation about the local Sunday bazaar in a nearby tea garden that we intend to visit before winding up our trip to this place.

"About Ana's story," I start speaking in the vernacular in order to exclude Ronnie from the conversation. "I've a question."

Dibakar looks in my direction.

"After that incident, she was still alive. And you said you loved her."

"What do you mean?" he looks at me with vague eyes. Says, "Look! You're grown up with English culture and environment, but in India, one can't marry a raped woman."

'Why?"

"Society doesn't accept it."

"So you abandoned her?"

"I didn't marry her. I didn't marry anyone else either!" he says. "Afterall, I've to live in the society. And look, this is my real life story, and still I've shared it with you and that's because of Renu; and Renu being Ana's friend."

"I've a connection to this story," I declare.

"What?" he says. "I know Renu had married a doctor about that time and they then migrated to UK in late eighties. But I don't know if she knows that Ana died within a year after this incident."

"She knows. We all know that Ana committed suicide," I say, firm.

The firmness of my tone startles him a little.

"I want to know something else."

"What?" he says, his eyes gazing penetratingly.

"Do you know that Ana gave birth to a baby in my father's hospital before she disappeared in the railway track to get rid of her life made miserable by you?"

His jaw tightens as he clenches his teeth hard.

"I heard about that later, after her death."

"I need to ask you something."

His look turns into a deep question.

"Who else can be the father of the baby besides you?"

"The rapists."

He probably wouldn't answer any further questions and asks me to leave immediately.

The weight of his words made me very heavy and I sit there resting my head on my palms, eyes staring ahead.

He too goes to sit on a lone chair in the backyard. Takes a few puffs from the *hukkah*. And in a while, walks away. Lifting my backpack, I stand up and walk out of the gate. I walk out of the house. Walk out of the kind of life lived in those parts of the world. Ronnie follows me.

Once out on the lane, I wrap a loving hand around Ronnie's shoulders. Spotting a thicket of orchid on a roadside areca tree, I show him.

"Foxtail orchids," he says. A thin cobra slithers in around the tentacles of roots in slow motion, and Ronnie gets busy with his camera. I take a fag out of my pocket as I fight the tears.

Back on the highway, with music of 'Michael Learns to Rock' playing on the car stereo, we drive away under the arch of an open sky with vast fields of paddy in various shades of green on both sides of the road. At a distance, beyond a paddy field, a train moves like a giant caterpillar. After a drive of half an hour, green swells of tea bushes come into sight with women labourers with baskets on their backs deftly plucking tea leaves. As we reach the tea estate entrance way, a garden clerk whose name is Happy, joins us as a local journalist has arranged. He takes us for a stroll along the narrow walkways of textured loam that cut through the garden. A few alleys lead to the tea-tribe village dotted with huts where Happy chats up with a few young girls in their local dialect introducing them to us and making them break into a brief folk dance to the beats of music from a transistor in his hands. They dance briefly with precision of footwork, clasping each other's waist. Another woman with a nose pin as heavy as a bangle, demonstrates how they pluck tea leaves from the bushes: two to three young leaves with a tiny bud in between.

We then enter the Sunday bazaar where there's a gathering of men and women. For sale there are heaps of dry fish, vegetables, rice, pulses, and corpulent hillocks of pork oozing with blood. And, there are sumptuous displays of bright glass bangles, clothes with tinsel work, bamboo tankards, and culinary items. I see a few fedora hats of Birina weed on sale. I pick one for my father. Ronnie spots a man selling earrings and bracelets of animal bones and bird feathers and also a couple of tiger nail pendants. He starts communicating with them taking pictures and recording an occasional video. Two men walk past us with a cage with inebriated birds called bulbul birds for a fight.

I sit there letting my inner turmoil drown in the noise of the market: the screams of swine getting slaughtered, restless clucking of cocks from a cockerel-fight and cheer of people watching a bulbul fight in progress. I buy a *biri* from a stall, and smoke quietly in the hullaballoo of the bazaar. My mind goes whirling around the previous day's story of my mother. Then, outdoing all the noise of the market, movie songs start flowing from an auto rickshaw with an attached loud speaker. The ruthless loudness blocks all my thoughts and I cover my ears with both hands.

We walk into a concrete box like structure – a tea stall it is. I choose to sit on a bench at the rear end of the rows of tables and chairs where the window shows a good view of the sprawling tea garden greens. As Ronnie and Happy exchange ideas through multiple layers of communication – verbal, written and sign language, I sit there not sure feeling like what. I close my eyes and feel the backdrop sounds blur away and my mind levitate slowly, as the wind sway the shedding trees of the garden underneath. I close my eyes and feel myself breeze through. In an Amphetamine-like haze, I dwell there sliding above the sprawls of greens with the sun shining through the trees giving the garden a mysterious dappled look.

My cell phone starts ringing and that snaps me back to the moment.

"Hello." It's Louni's voice. "Uncle Dibakar is on his way to meet you in the market," her words startle me. "He'll be there in fifteen minutes. Please wait for him in the Saalonibari tea stall."

My mind goes berserk beneath a heart full of woes. I find no formed responses or reactions in me; with a numb mind I join the chat that has been going on between Ronnie and Happy and his people. Outside the door, a man totters out of a shack restaurant of country beer, a few people sit playing canasta cards on the ground.

One of Happy's friends comes over with a plate of fries – the recipe of which he goes on to explain, "It is made of young tea leaves smeared with a spicy batter of rice flour and deep fried in drops."

I sit there popping a couple of the fries. Then I arrange our papers and CDs into the right folders of my backpack when I see Dibakar get down from a bike at a distance; his dhoti tightly wrapped around his thigh above the knees, feet in thick leather sandals and a scarf around his neck. He casts around the place wearing an anxious look. With my mind still numb, I wave my hand at him. Locating me, as he starts walking in my way my heart starts pounding in my chest; I arrange my thoughts into some kind of an agreeable conversation. Dibakar walks in. I rise as he approaches me with intense yet soulful eyes, and, then he raises one of his hands to put it on my shoulder.

***